DREAMING THE BEAR

Mimi Thebo

 Published in the United States by Wendy Lamb Books, an imprint of Random House Children's Books, a division of Penguin Random House LLC, New York.
Originally published in the UK by Oxford University Press in 2016.

Wendy Lamb Books and the colophon are trademarks of Penguin Random House LLC.

Visit us on the Web! randomhouseteens.com

Educators and librarians, for a variety of teaching tools, visit us at RHTeachersLibrarians.com

Library of Congress Cataloging-in-Publication Data
Names: Thebo, Mimi, author.
Title: Dreaming the bear / Mimi Thebo.
Description: First edition. | New York : Wendy Lamb Books, an imprint of Random House Children's Books, [2017] | Originally published: Oxford : Oxford University Press, 2016. | Summary: "Set in Yellowstone National Park, teenager Darcy has moved with her family from England to the U.S. She's been sick and has strange dreams/visions. Then she finds an injured bear. The bear and Darcy need each other. But is Darcy well enough to take care of the bear, let alone herself?"—Provided by publisher.
Identifiers: LCCN 2016011178 (print) | LCCN 2016038643 (ebook) | ISBN 978-0-399-55750-7 (trade) | ISBN 978-0-399-55751-4 (lib. bdg.) | ISBN 978-0-399-55753-8 (pbk.) | ISBN 978-0-399-55752-1 (eBook)
Subjects: | CYAC: Grizzly bear—Fiction. | Bears—Fiction. | Human-animal relationships—Fiction. | Sick—Fiction. | British—United States—Fiction. | Yellowstone National Park—Fiction.
Classification: LCC PZ7.1.T448 Dr 2017 (print) | LCC PZ7.1.T448 (ebook) | DDC [Fic]—dc23

The text of this book is set in 12.5-point Bell.
Interior design by Ken Crossland

Printed in the United States of America
10 9 8 7 6 5 4 3 2 1
First American Edition

For Andy and Libs
(with thanks also to Courtney, Izzy,
Molly, Sophia, Foyle, and Bear 134)

Chapter One

Everything is quiet. I can hear my raspy breath getting rougher with every step of these stupid snowshoes. Then I hear something else—a bird, maybe. But I can't see where it is. All I see is pine trees in every direction. And snow, of course.

I wonder when I can go back. How long has it been? But I don't want to peel down my warm, padded mitten to look at my watch. The cold air attacks any little weakness, like a bare wrist. It seems like it's trying to get at you. As if it's personal.

And anyway, it's only been about five minutes since the last time I looked.

I'm supposed to be out here for two to four hours every day, to build up my lungs. The doctor said cold won't do me any harm, if I'm dressed for it. He said I should take care not to get wet.

There's a hill I haven't been up. I've always taken the ways that go around it. Today I am so bored, I'll try to go uphill and see if there's anything interesting up there. I know I shouldn't go uphill, but I do it anyway. If my muscles really start hurting, I'll stop, right?

My dad spends all day out in the cold, and even some nights. When he talks about his fieldwork, I don't listen. Evidently, finding out about deer populations with natural predators is so important that we had to move to the middle of a giant wilderness. Nothing is that important. It wasn't worth it.

If I was home, I could walk to the library. I could wander through our little town's high street, looking in all the junk shops. I could go swimming— No, I couldn't, because I'm not supposed to get wet.

But if I was home, I *could* get wet, because I wouldn't have gotten pneumonia in the first place. I wouldn't have been in the hospital for three weeks. I wouldn't be all skinny and run-down and weak. I'd be at a real school, with people who actually *like* me. I'd be with my friends.

I wouldn't be with gung-ho lunatics like Susan Hackmeyer, who thinks she knows everything. She doesn't. She only knows stuff about being *here.* She couldn't find her way across London by Tube, like I had to do last year. She couldn't spot the next big hit song. Just because I can't tell the difference between deer poo and elk poo, she tried to make me look stupid in front of Tony Infante.

As if I needed any help to look stupid in front of Tony Infante.

I get so upset thinking about all this that I am halfway up the hill, which was a lot steeper than it looked, before my lungs hurt and I notice my breath has gone all noisy and harsh. I really need to stop walking uphill. My legs are burning. But then I see where I am.

I can't stop. If I stop, I'll fall about thirty feet, straight down.

You shoe up steep hills sideways, kind of like making stairs for yourself in the snow. It's hard. Stopping means balancing, and that's tricky. I have poles to help, but I haven't been taking them lately. They seem heavy.

My poles are still on the porch of the cabin.

I've just been cutting into this hill, letting my anger carry me up. And now, when I need one of the millions and trillions of pine trees in this *stupid* wilderness, there's not a single one I can actually reach and hold on to so that I can rest. I have to keep moving or I'll fall.

All the time I'm thinking about this, my feet keep on cutting little steps and I keep huffing up the hill.

It hurts so bad that my lungs start to ache, too.

All my big muscles are burning now—not just my legs, but my bottom and my arms and back too. The doctor explained why this happens. Muscles need oxygen to flush out the lactic acid that builds up when I exercise. Since my lungs are still crinkly and wet, I'm not making enough oxygen to flush them.

Which is why I'm not supposed to go uphill.

It doesn't help that my lungs are used to being at sea level and I'm living at more than six thousand feet above it. That's one of the reasons I got pneumonia in the first place. I'm not adjusting well to the altitude. And it doesn't help to think of this about a million times a day and get angry at my dad every time, either. Emotional upset isn't good for my breathing, apparently.

I'm hurting really badly, and the brow of the hill is twenty steps away. I glance, and it's a long way down. I wish I hadn't glanced.

I'm getting black spots in front of my eyes. I'm fighting off weird thoughts—like maybe I could roll back down. Or that it would be nice to just die and not hurt anymore.

It was so stupid to try to climb this hill.

And then I get the faraway thing again, when I'm kind of outside me and looking down. As if I'm up somewhere civilized, like a space station, and I'm zooming in on Earth and America and Montana and the wilderness and the park and zooming, zooming right in to our area, and our cabin and me, halfway up this horrible hill.

I'm like a black-and-red dot moving up a white page. As

soon as you can tell it's a person, you can tell I'm a girl. Even in my padded clothes, I'm thin. My shining brown ponytail trembles with every movement.

I waver. My knees sink, and for a moment I look as though I might fall. But then I half climb, half stagger to the brow of the hill and then collapse into the snow.

What do bears dream? What do they want?

The bear dreams of her cubs. They sleep against her, in the long time of dark and cold. In her sleep she moves her great arm to gather them close.

Somewhere in her mind a deep reflex: they are not there. The cubs are not where they should be. There is cold where there should be warmth.

She swims up from her heaviness. She feels the dryness of her mouth and opens one eye.

She remembers the last time she saw the cubs. The things the men did. She feels the memory in the pain of her shoulder. Would the thought of leaving her cubs hurt, too? Maybe more? She closes her eye and groans, rolling on her back to her other side, away from the cave's opening and the place her cubs used to lie.

Snow begins to fall.

I lie in the snow for a long time, long enough for the thick white flakes to cover the red patches of my coat.

When I sit up, I look at my watch, but I don't see it. I still see me, from a long way away. I am shivering. I crawl to the brow of the hill and look down the steep slope. Part of me notices how far it is, and part of me watches me noticing.

I try to get to my feet, but I am shaking. My knees fold underneath me, and I sit down, hard. My ponytail is dark with melted snow.

Wet, I notice. I got wet. I'm not supposed to get wet.

I look the other way and see a shelter of sorts—a low cave in the rocks of the hill. I crawl inside.

It is dark, and I shiver hard. One of my snowshoes drags behind me, half off my boot. My eyes are pulling shut when I sense warmth and lean my back into it.

The bear half wakes again. Someone is there. Her sensitive nose tells her immediately that it is not her cubs, that it is not another bear. But under the perfumed shampoo and soap and deodorant, she smells another animal. Whatever it is, it is alive. And it is small and cold.

She rolls again, flings out her great arm, and drags the thing to her chest. She feels it warming beneath her touch.

Chapter Two

I close the door behind me super, super quietly and strip off my coat and overalls, shoving them straight into the washing machine. That's when I realize I've lost my hat.

My mother is at the big table, surrounded by books and papers. She's meant to finish her PhD in the two years we're in Montana, and my illness has disrupted everything. She missed a conference, and she had an important tutorial scheduled at the conference. Now she's getting ready to go to *another* conference, but she's behind on her research.

She says snowmobiling to Mammoth every time she needs WiFi is what's slowing her down, but really, it's been looking after me.

Her hair is standing on end, and she has a pencil between her teeth longways, pushing against the corners of her mouth. She keeps her eyes on her screen and says, "Igo woowy oo go . . . ," and then realizes she's not making any sense and takes out the pencil.

"I was worried about you in this snow. It's been nearly four hours! I was scared you'd get wet." She looks up and finally sees me, and her eyebrows fly up in line with her fair hair. "You *did* get wet! Darcy!" The way she says my name, you'd think I'd murdered somebody.

I shrug. "I lost my hat," I say, trying to act like it's no big deal. We do that a lot in our family.

She stands up and feels me all over. "Go use the hair dryer *immediately*," she scolds. "And then eat some soup."

And now that I'm in my bedroom, blow-drying, I know I'm not going to say anything about what happened. My dad would go ballistic if he knew I'd cuddled up to a hibernating grizzly. If I even did. If it wasn't a dream or some kind of hallucination. That whole seeing-myself-from-a-distance thing that happens lately when I'm feeling sick . . . that's a bit weird.

So it's not like I can trust my own mind. This place has driven me completely insane.

If my mum knew I'd nearly killed myself with over-exertion and hypothermia, she'd kill me. Her catch-up conference is in Chicago next week. It's only just now that I realize how selfish it was to go up that hill.

I'll just keep my little adventure to myself.

I go back downstairs. The soup is wonderful. A tomatoey something or other that Mum has made. I sit on the sofa with my legs up, under the green woolly blanket, drinking my soup and watching the little window in the woodburning stove dance with flame.

The next thing I know, my dad's rough hand is on my forehead. "She's fine," I hear him say. I keep my eyes shut. I don't want to talk to my dad.

"Oh, I know she's fine *now*. . . ." Mum's voice doesn't sound convinced.

"Pack," Dad says. "The snow coach driver has promised to come down the access road and pick you up here, but you have to be ready at dawn. If you don't get out before this storm, you won't get out at all."

I can feel my mother's eyes on me, and I try to look asleep. Inside, though, my heart begins to pound, and I can feel sweat starting up under my arms.

I'm not really ready for Mum to leave me. *I don't trust Dad to look after me*, I start to think, but then I stop myself.

That isn't fair. It's not Dad I don't trust, it's me.

"I'll be around," Dad says. "I won't just ski off for twelve hours. I won't forget that I'm holding the fort. And Jem will come home straight after school, too, instead of the observation hut or the office."

I can feel my mother's silence. It has objections in it that she's said too many times to have to say now. I'm not like my older brother, Jem. Dad can't treat me as if I'm a new recruit to his army unit. I'm not fitting in here. I need friends and television and radio and a phone signal and WiFi. Mum always says my natural habitat is the shopping mall and the multiplex. Dad used to laugh when she said it. And then we came here, and he didn't laugh anymore.

She just says my name. "Darcy . . ." And it has all that other stuff inside it.

And he says, "I know." And then he says, "Maybe . . ." And I know what's in that, too. I know he hopes I'll come around. That I'll suddenly enjoy the wilderness. That I'll stop being so inconveniently ill and unhappy and let him get on with his life.

Mum sighs. She says, "I wouldn't get my hopes up, Marcus."

I can sleep forever these days. It's all I want to do. I've only been pretending to sleep on the sofa, but I forget and go to sleep for real. The next thing I know, Mum is bumping her suitcase down the stairs.

I get up and help her. It weighs a ton.

She says, "There's a storm coming. If I don't get out this morning, the snowcoach won't be able to take me tomorrow." The snowcoach is what you'd get if a bus mated with a tank. It's got seats inside and places for luggage, but it's also got big tracks instead of wheels.

Her hair is all clean and shiny and straight. Mum looks ready to go, but her eyes look worried behind her glasses.

I say, "I know." And when she hugs me, I say, "I'll be all right." That's what all of us say in my family, no matter what's actually happening: *I'll be all right, it'll be fine.*

In our family, we don't cling to our mother and whimper and beg her to give up on her work so that we won't have to be sick without her. So when I say, "I'll be all right," it's not because it's true, it's because I don't know what else there is to say. I haven't been taught any other words.

She's telling me something about a big quiche she made for me last night and how it will be nice warmed up for breakfast when I hear the snowcoach coming. Jem runs down the stairs in a T-shirt and boxer shorts, and jams on a polar fleece and his Sorel boots to take her suitcase out to it. She keeps hugging me. I have to push her away and out the door. I can see the driver getting tense, waiting, and Jem's out there, practically naked in the cold, standing next to the big tanklike track-wheels. Tourists are looking out curiously.

I promise I'll eat. I promise I'll be careful. I promise I'll do my best to get on with Dad and Jem. Someone called Nancy is coming around to do some housework. The phone numbers are by Mum's bed. I'm to call the doctor if I feel even the least bit sick.

I stand in the doorway and nod and nod and promise. And then I wave and wave and smile and wave. And then I pull Jem past the door.

"Don't be an idiot," I tell him. "You'll get pneumonia."

* * *

Dad is pacing around the room. It's not even ten a.m. His work is spread out on the table—laptop, external hard drive, and pages and pages of observation notes. But he keeps looking out the window.

"How's your book?" he asks.

It would be better if I could read it in peace, I think. "Fine," I say.

"Do you want another cup of tea?"

"No." Then I remember that one of my promises was to be nice to Dad. "Thanks."

He looks out the window again. "I think the storm is going to hold off until this afternoon. Jem will probably be able to stay at school the whole day." He clears his throat. "It looks like we've got lots of time before it hits."

I am reading. This is a book here. And I am reading it. I say nothing.

He says, "Darcy?"

Here it comes. "Yes?"

"When are you going to take your air?"

I look at him. I don't need to say how little I want to go and take my air. I guess I have things in my silences too. I'd never really thought about it before.

He sighs. He says, "Darcy. It's important."

I hedge a bit. "Do you really think the storm will hold off?"

"There's blue skies."

Oh, God. I thought I'd be able to rest today. "Well," I say, "I should probably go now, while it's sunny."

"Would you like to come over to the observation hut with me?" he said. "I hate to waste the weather."

I can't ski. I mean, I can ski, of course. But I still fall over a lot. And the doctor said that I wasn't to get wet, so that means I shouldn't fall over in the snow. So right now, I'm not supposed to ski. I say, "But . . ."

And Dad says, "It's okay. We can shoe over there."

It'll take forever. I'll be shoeing for about an hour there and an hour back. I'll be utterly exhausted. I say, "No. I'd just hold you up. You go." And when he pauses, I say, "I'll just shoe around nearer the house, in case I get tired."

He looks at me. He says, "Well, you were out a long time yesterday."

Yes, and I nearly killed myself, I think.

He says, "Right. We'll go out in . . . what? Twenty minutes. And I will meet you back here in exactly two hours. Unless it starts to snow, in which case I'll race you home. Deal?"

He holds out his hand to be slapped. I raise my eyebrows. "Deal," I say, but I don't slap it.

I wonder if I can control the whole seeing-myself-from-the-outside thing. If it's part of my illness or if I'm just really good at imagining. I decide to give it a try while Dad is there, while we are getting ready to go. I picture the cabin, how it must look from above . . .

The house in the snow. Only a thin thread of smoke curls from the roof, like an old man smoking a pipe out in the sun.

The stillness of a winter pine forest explodes with noise as the door bangs open. The air itself feels startled and affronted, and any tiny rustlings in the forest stop instantly. Anyone who is listening immediately understands that all of winter nature has been frightened.

The man in dirty white camouflage is not listening. He slams his boots into his ski bindings and settles his pack and his rifle over his shoulders. He speaks loudly and jovially to me, sitting down on the front porch, fiddling with my snow shoes. My lavender hat clashes with my coat and hair.

The man is poling away when he stops and effortlessly slides to turn and shout, "See if you can find your hat! It was expensive!" before spinning on one ski and gliding away.

I stick out my tongue at the man's back. I waddle off the porch and begin to stump heavily away.

Chapter Three

How many words would a bear have for sleep?

As the morning wears on, she finds herself leaving the well of coma and swimming up through unconsciousness to a heavy drowse. Bear is expecting something. Bear is waiting.

I have no intention of going back to the cave. It would be stupid—worse than stupid. Suicidal. Mum would never forgive herself for leaving if I died in the cave today.

I look for my red hat.

I hurt everywhere, and I am so, so tired. Why didn't

I just pretend to go out and then go back to sleep by the fire? Dad would never know.

I guess I actually want to get better and stop feeling like I'm stuck in a giant marshmallow. I'm sick of plodding along in this white world, where my feet stick and everything pulls against me.

How hard can it be to find a red hat in the snow? I'm pretty sure I had it going up. It would have fallen off when I was all dozy and going back to the cabin. I can't even remember that bit.

I look carefully on both sides of the trail, but in no time, I'm at the bottom of the hill.

I have no intention of going up the hill. I have not planned to go back to the cave. But then, I did bring my poles. . . .

It's so much easier going up now that I've already cut the stairs and have my poles. I'm up in less than half the time it took yesterday. But my lungs still sound horrible as I gasp for air at the top. I have to work hard not to let myself flop in the snow again. And as I gasp, I get that faraway feeling. . . .

. . . I lean my hands on my knees and breathe raggedly. When I straighten I waver on my feet. I am drawn to the cave. My arms and legs seem to fall away behind me, almost as if I am floating, stomach-first, on an invisible current of air. I'm some new species of Gore-Tex jellyfish, blowing through the atmosphere on the faintest of breezes, being sucked into the depths of a dark, draining sea.

The bear raises her arm, and I am the little cold creature that crawls into warmth. Together we dive down into a dreamworld. The bear feels a catch in her breath, smells the antiseptic air of the pulmonary ward. I feel the sting of the bullet, the ripped shoulder. We mourn the ones who are lost, the love, the light, and the summer.

"Why do you keep washing your coat and overalls?"

Dad doesn't notice when I'm hungry. He doesn't notice when I'm sad. But he notices that I've washed my outer layers twice in two days.

I say, "They smelled bad." Which is true, but not as true as "They reeked of grizzly bear." Of the two, though, I think I've said the one he'd most like to hear.

Dad thinks about this. It's one of the things I used to like about him, the way he takes his time to think about what you've said. He is tall and blond, and his forehead crinkles up when he thinks. I remember loving him, but it feels like a long time ago. Now when I watch him think, I only feel an echo of it.

He says, "It's a bit of a waste. Next time, hang them outside to freshen. I'll anchor some carabiners to the porch, so they won't blow away if it storms."

This is typical Dad. If you have a problem, equipment will help you solve it. Ideally, something we already have, like the metal D ring of a connector called "a carabiner." He has got millions of them in the climbing kit, but every time we get to an outdoor shop, he'll look at all the carabiners, as if there might have been some startling new technological innovation since the last time he went in.

He looks at his watch and then out the window. It's starting to snow, and Jem isn't home yet. I've filled the kettle, and it's on the stove, starting to steam, but there's still no Jem.

Back home, if Jem was late, we'd think he'd stopped to buy junk food or was browsing the used games at the place on the corner. Now we think he might have dropped into a ravine or missed the orange-topped poles and lost himself in the endless trees.

And then we hear the whine of the snowmobile. Dad sits down and tries to look like he'd been working and not standing at the window worrying over Jem. That's a boy thing. They can't look as though they do things like that. I put tea bags into the pot and biscuits onto a plate.

Jem always fills up a room. He is big and blond, like Dad. He's handsome and clever and good at everything he does. We'd been here exactly three weeks when he won a log-splitting contest. He's already on the cross-country-skiing team. He's like that.

I've spent my life trying to keep up with Jem.

I've always failed.

And now that I'm so sick and weak, I've given up. Just watching him makes me feel tired. I don't look at him when he comes in.

So it's a surprise to hear the other voice.

I don't remember much about school. I got sick right after we moved here. It was just a cold then, but I was so unhappy and ill that I was kind of in my own little world. Jem keeps coming home and talking about his day and saying I must remember this person or that person, but I don't remember very many of the kids who go to the little high school.

But I remember one. He's dark and thin, with black hair and green eyes. And I fell in love the moment I met him.

"You know Tony, don't you?" my brother asks. Tony Infante looks at me shyly, and smiles.

Dad has this horrible habit of answering questions people are actually asking me. I usually hate it. But just then I'm happy that Dad says "Sure" and stands up to shake hands. Jem's eyes meet mine and he shrugs, sorry that Dad's done it again, assumed that I can't, or don't need to, speak for myself.

For some reason, this afternoon, Jem's kindness makes my eyes sting, and for a moment I think I might burst into tears, right then and there, in front of Tony Infante.

"We're Tony's weather plan," Jem says. "Mum signed the form so that we're his storm residence. His people live even farther out."

"My father is Matt Infante," Tony says, as if that explains something. And it does, to Dad.

Dad says, "Ah," in a don't-bother-to-tell-me-more-because-I-know-everything kind of way. I bring the tea tray with an extra mug to the table.

They talk about the weather. The snow is coming down hard, and the wind is starting to pick up. It's meant to be the biggest storm of the year.

Outside the window is still bright, but it's getting dark in the house. Jem gets up and turns on the lamps.

At last, Dad remembers to make dinner. Jem and Tony go up to Jem's room.

I sit at the table and watch the whirling snow. It's coming from all directions, blowing up from the ground and from side to side and still coming down hard from up above. If you were out in this, you wouldn't be able to find your way. You'd only know which way was down because you could feel the earth under your boots. People have died just yards away from their houses. They went out to get some wood or something and never found their way back to the door.

Dad is frying an onion. He seems to know what he is doing.

I go up to change my top and brush my hair.

It exhausts me.

Bending down to open a drawer. Stripping off one top, pulling on another. Walking to the wash basket. Bending down to close the drawer. Raising my arms above my head to brush my hair.

Instead of going back down the stairs, I sit on my

bed, propping myself up on the pillows. Finally, I forget about the idea of sitting again and pull my heavy legs after me.

Next door, I can hear Jem and Tony talking. They don't chatter away nonstop. You do that with people you like but you don't know very well. They sound like proper friends. There are long periods of silence, and then one of them will share something with the other, and they'll talk about it or laugh. And then they'll go back to doing whatever they were doing, separately but side by side, until there's something else to share.

And the rhythm of this reminds me of something so painful that I curl into a ball.

Sue.

All my other friends have faded in my mind to a picture of sunshine and laughter and warmth. Of course, I can still picture Izzy and Sophia and Molly and the rest in my mind, but I can't picture them apart. I see them in one joyous gang. I see them from the center of that gang. I am the white shadow in the picture.

It's different with Sue.

I don't remember her a hundred times a day. A hundred times a day, I get close to remembering her and stop myself because it hurts so bad. Ever since I got sick, I write her an email once a week, and it's rubbish. I download it onto a USB, and Dad takes it in to the nearest Internet connection in Mammoth, sends it, and brings me the ones she writes back. They're brilliant—

like she's talking to me. And this whole process is so terribly painful that I haven't started it up again since I got out of the hospital.

How can I describe Sue? I could write a thousand words describing Sue's left eyebrow. I know every hair of it, know how it curves slightly differently from her right eyebrow. Sue and I were at nursery together, and then primary school, and then we went to Jem's school. Sue is not just my friend. She is part of me. Leaving her felt like I was getting ripped in half.

I reach under the bed and take out a brightly wrapped box.

I don't know why I didn't open her Christmas present. At first I said I wanted to open it by myself. And then I said I was saving it. And now it's after Easter, and it's kind of dusty and faded-looking.

I hear Jem and Tony talk again and then fall silent together again. And finally, I decide I can't hurt anymore, and it's time to open the present.

The paper sounds loud to me when I rip it, and I have some trouble getting the ribbon off.

It's a box. It's a big, pretty, pinky-purple box. And she's decorated it. She's pasted pictures of us together and my mates and my favorite pop stars and actors all over it. And she's put ribbon on it and flowers and got somebody to varnish it, so it's smooth and bright and really wonderful. It glows on my bed.

There's a particularly strong gust of wind outside,

and the whole cabin sways a little. My window is just a white square. You can't even see snow anymore.

On my bed, the box seems to pulse with color, like neon.

And this hurts, but kind of in a good way, a way I can take. I have tears leaking down my face, but I'm happy. I'm happy knowing she loves me and misses me, too. Even though I knew it before.

After I've looked at it awhile, I open the box. I don't know what I was expecting.

It's everything. Sue has sent me *supplies.*

Strawberry sweets and Dairy Milk Buttons. A CD, because she knows I can't download music. No, two CDs, no . . . three! And three DVDs. A makeup case with sparkly eye shadow, and lipstick. A fake-nails kit. Pedicure jewels. Fake-tan cream. A highlighting kit. Little things you put in your bra to make your breasts look bigger (we'd always wanted those). Four bottles of nail varnish in all my favorite colors. A really grown-up bra and panty set. A thin little black T-shirt with "Diva" written in rhinestones on the front. Little notes on heart-shaped paper from all my friends, saying they love me and miss me.

I suddenly realize my door is open. Jem and Tony and Dad are all looking at me. Dad's got an oven glove on and a spatula in his hand.

I blink at them like I've never seen them before.

"You were screaming," Jem says.

"More like squealing," Tony says. "I think."

They all come closer and take a look at some of the stuff that's in the box. Thank goodness none of them notice the plastic things you put in your bra.

Dad says, "I feel like I should lecture you about the throwaway culture and how materialism is destroying Earth. But it's the first time I've seen you smile in months."

Tony is looking at the bottle of navy-blue nail varnish. "I wouldn't mind wearing this," he says.

Dinner is pretty good. And afterward Tony and I paint our nails navy blue. Jem tries one finger, but he cleans it off immediately. When my nails dry, I write Sue a huge long thank-you email, telling her all about the blizzard and the way the cabin shakes and how I have to snowshoe every day. I have just saved it onto the USB when the power goes out.

We still have our woodburning stove downstairs, but there's no electricity to run the central heating. Tony tells us it could be days before it comes back on.

We have drilled about what to do. We all have quick showers while the water is still hot. And then we pack up boxes of everything in our rooms that could be damaged by freezing and store them in the big cupboard downstairs. I add my beautiful box from Sue. We take out enough clothes for four or five days. And then we seal up the doors to our rooms with special insulating tape. Dad drains the toilet tank and the hot-water tank and shuts off the water to the upstairs. We'll have to pump up water from the well. We'll have to use the embarrassing little bathroom downstairs, where everyone can hear you do a poo.

While Dad does that, Jem and Tony and I move the big table against the kitchen island. We'll just have to sit closer together.

We move the sofa the other way, against the wall, and get out the sleeping pads and bags, lining them up on the rug. When Dad comes down, he tells us we've done it all just right.

Then Tony remembers about the fridge and the freezer. We put everything that needs to stay cool on the windowsills, and everything that needs to stay frozen in big, animal-proof canisters outside.

Dad goes out on the porch and attaches them to the special bolts. He is right outside the window, but we can hardly see him.

When he comes back in, his beard is matted with snow and ice. He says he had to feel his way to the door.

Tomorrow, he and Jem have to go to the woodpile. They'll take the sled and haul a lot of wood back, even though it's only around the side of the house. We have a cup of tea while we plan how we'll do this. Tony and I will be on the porch. Jem and Dad will wear climbing harnesses and rope while they're off to the porch, so that they don't get lost. I will bang pots and pans when they blow a whistle to say they are coming back, and Tony will pull in the slack on the rope.

Dad is worried because I washed my hair and it's still damp. We move the sleeping bags so that I am closer to the living room log burner. Then we stoke up both burners, use the embarrassing toilet, and brush our teeth together at the kitchen sink.

It's all actually kind of fun. When I lie down, I even stay awake for a minute or two and look at the fire.

Chapter Four

How does a sleeping bear sense weather? Her paw is over her face. Does her sensitive nose smell the snow? Does she feel the drop in pressure in her lungs and kidneys?

Deeper and deeper into sleep she sinks. Her heartbeat slows to an unimaginably faint pulse. Her diaphragm rises and falls as a slow ripple of muscle, and her lungs never inflate—they only whisper a bird's breath up and a bird's breath down.

She is gone beyond dreams, deep into the pea at the top of her spinal cord. Everything else she is, is gone. She is little more than a collection of cells. One slightly too-slow beat or one bird's breath too few, and the collection will break free. What was once the bear will dissipate into the air and the earth of the cave.

To survive she must go to this fine line between life and death and make her bed on it. And she cannot doubt herself. She must be certain that she is able to do this, to surrender to the deepest, most unknowable part of herself, or she will never be able to sink down, down to where she uses nearly nothing and survives.

Four people sleep in a neat row. Three are still. The one nearest the cold window is troubled by dreams. His arms struggle against the restraint of his sleeping bag, as if he is fighting it, as if it is trying to kill him.

I see myself slit open my eyes. Something about the night and the storm and the cold has made it easy for me to slip out of my body and watch from above.

It's not the first time I've woken to Dad's nightmares. "Soldiers have nightmares," Mum used to say. "Even when they aren't soldiers anymore." He sits up and passes a shaking hand across his beard.

He moves quietly, though he is so large. The door of the woodburning stove creaks open, and he places three more logs, carefully, one by one, on the burning coals. After he creaks the door shut and checks the latch, he moves carefully and silently to where I am. He sits and watches me, looks closely at the rise and fall of my breathing, the color in my cheek. My hair is tangled over my forehead, and he can't see my open eyes.

And then he does something strange. He passes his hands above my body—once, twice, three times. Tenderly, as if he were stroking me and not just the air. Then he sits and watches me some more as the storm batters the curtained window and shakes the log walls.

I come back into my body and hear him. He's doing something I didn't think he did. He's praying.

The first day is fun. We all get very silly after our successful log-gathering operation. I guess it's because we know we have everything we need to ride out the storm and we don't have any more responsibilities.

We make loads of popcorn on top of the woodstove and play board games on the floor. During a Monopoly game, my dad loses all his hotels and houses and rolls around on the floor, having a fake tantrum. I laugh until my lungs hurt, and when they do, he looks at me sharply, and I remember the night before, the two of us awake in the storm.

I fall asleep playing gin rummy, worn out from laughing so hard.

When I wake up they've laid me on the sofa and covered me with a green blanket. Something beany-smelling is cooking in the big iron pot on the kitchen stove. I feel so safe and so looked-after that I can't get out of my body.

I go back to sleep again and don't wake up until it's time to eat.

The second day of the storm, Dad has to go out the special roof window and push the snow off the roof. He and Jem don't want any help. Jem's job is to keep the rope taut, and Dad has to walk around and push off the snow with the special red shovel. The snow has been accumulating fast up there because the central heating is off.

I am worried about them up there, a bit, but I have my own job to do.

Tony and I clean the downstairs. It really needs it, with four of us living in one big room and all using the little toilet.

Tony tells me stories about roofs collapsing and people who ran out of food. He tells me stories about people getting lost in storms.

And then he tells me a story about a man who sheltered with a sleeping bear.

I feel my heart catch a beat and rise up to my throat. I don't trust my voice to ask any more about it, but Tony seems to sense that I'm interested in that one and tells me all he knows. Which isn't much.

But still.

It's good to know it's not just me.

I make a big, hot pasta dish for lunch. Jem and Dad are quiet, and I feel like something happened up there on the roof. But Tony keeps everybody talking.

It's like he knows something happened, and he knows I am worried. I look at his green eyes, and he is sliding them from one of us to the other, as if he is checking on us all. His white teeth are flashing, and his perfect lips are chattering away, but I can tell he knows what he's doing and that he's trying to take care of everyone.

He's like that.

And I want to get up and stand behind him and hold his head against my stomach and stroke his glossy black hair and tell him not to worry about us, that we'll be okay.

But of course I can't do anything like that.

So I try to look really happy, like I'm not worried about what went on upstairs.

Tony's dad was in charge of reintroducing the wolf population to the park. He got death threats, and had a security detail for a while. Tony tells us a bit about what it was like, and Dad gets *really* interested and starts talking to us all again.

And pretty soon they are talking about some big meeting and who was on which side. Dad even gets out his notebook and begins writing things down. So Jem and I clear the table.

I bump into Jem's arm by the sink, and he winces. His arm has a long rope burn. He shows me, and I go and get the arnica from the first-aid box. He winces again when it goes on, too. It must really hurt—Jem's usually pretty stoic.

I wash the dishes while Jem dries, and I ask, "What happened on the roof?"

If I push Jem to tell me, he won't. So I just wash dishes, waiting, waiting for Jem to decide to tell me more.

It works. Jem says, "It's not that acute of a slope, and the wind was steady, and he had his crampons." Jem dries a bit more, and I wait *forever* for Jem to say what he's worried about. Finally: "I think Dad is starting to get old."

"He's only fifty-one," I say. "He's really fit. He's fitter than anybody I know." I think about the time he had some friends cycling through Nepal to raise money for some charity. One of them broke his leg skiing just before the trip, so Dad stepped in with five days' notice. He was one of only three of them to finish the course, and he hadn't even done any training. I say, "Remember Nepal?"

"That was five years ago," Jem says. "He would have *fallen off the roof,* Darcy."

And landed in the nice, soft snow, I think as the storm steadily blows white against the north windows. Or maybe landed across the woodpile or on his head. With no telephone to call the doctor. With no way to get him to the hospital. The south windows look both white and dark at the same time, like it's not just snow out there, like there's something in the shadows.

I thought I'd be less worried if I knew, but now I'm more worried. I've never really thought about how much we need Dad. He's always just been there.

Jem's eyes are big and round. And suddenly I know this is the first time Jem understands that Dad is an actual human, too. That Dad is mortal. Jem's older than I am, but sometimes he's . . . well, he's kind of thick.

I think I love Jem more when he's stupid like this than when he's being superboy. I give him a cuddle, and he wraps his arms around me and holds me close.

And something about the way he holds me reminds me of the bear.

It's the third day of the storm, and there is nothing to do but live through it.

We've got water and wood, and the roof is okay.

We get very tidy. We fight over who gets to clean out the ashes from the stove and have to settle it with rock, scissors, paper. We use dice to draw up a list of who is in charge of what for the duration of the storm.

There's three or four jobs each. Dad gets cooking. Jem gets stoking fires. Those are the big ones. I get cleaning the toilet, putting dishes away and airing bedding. Tony is in charge of cleaning all surfaces, washing dishes, and fresh air. Every once in a while, he opens a window a tiny crack, and the storm blows into the room.

We had beans yesterday, and we're all making horrible smells. At first I thought I would die of shame doing a fart in front of Tony Infante, but we're all doing it. A lot. Tony's jumping up quite a bit to open and close the window.

It is the fourth day of the storm, and Dad and Jem make me learn how to unload, strip, clean, reassemble, and reload a rifle. I do time trials with Tony, and I win two out of five. I suspect he's letting me win.

The rest of the day, we read. Dad catches up on all the paperwork he can do without charging his laptop. Tony says that's how all the paperwork in the park gets done and that his dad has four spare laptop batteries that he charges whenever the weather looks bad. Tony and I do our nails again, and Dad lets me give him a pedicure. I use bright pink.

Mum should have been home today.

The fifth day I wake up shivering in the dark. The fire has gone out. I call out, "Jem. Jem," but he doesn't hear me. I feel so bad, I start to cry.

I start to move out of my body, but I'm scared to do that. I hold on to myself, and it makes me tired.

Then Dad is there, holding me, and Jem is moving fast and saying sorry a lot. Tony takes over making the fire because Jem is so upset he's doing it wrong. I keep trying to tell him it's okay, but my teeth are chattering so hard I can't make him understand.

Dad is kind to Jem, but I can hear Jem crying, and it makes my heart hurt.

The fire blazes up, and Dad lays me right in front

of it. He unzips my sleeping bag and crawls in with me, and Tony heaps the other bags on top of us. I am not allowed to go to sleep. They keep making me sing along to Disney songs until I warm up, and Jem has made a big pot of tea.

The snow has finally stopped, but it is very, very cold.

Jem brings in more wood, and Dad inspects the house for insulation leaks and lays out the little solar panel to charge the big radio. When he tells Tony he thinks it's too cold to snowmobile Tony home, Tony says, "No duh."

For some reason this makes us all laugh.

Dad keeps saying "no duh" to himself and chuckling all day.

Finally, in the afternoon, the big two-way radio crackles to life. Tony talks to his dad, who tells him to stay put. He warns that the temperature will drop even lower in the night. He tells us that trees are exploding from the cold.

It's really dangerous in the forest right now.

And anyway, another storm will hit tomorrow afternoon. We ask the park officials to send Mum a message: we are fine, and we still have lots of food.

Dad has to bother about twenty people to talk to the doctor, who is stuck at home, like everybody else.

Everybody talks about me like I'm some kind of freak. "Oh, your sick little girl," one of the park people says. I want to curl up and die with the shame of it.

Dad tells the doctor about me getting so cold and about being stuck in this room with two woodburners and a bunch of oil lamps. The doctor says it should be warmer in the morning. If I could get out for a while and take some light exercise, it would be good for me, as long as I stay dry and am well wrapped up.

Then the doctor reminds Dad in a very stern voice what he means by light exercise. I decide I do like the doctor, after all. Dad's idea of light exercise is skiing ten miles.

Right before supper we get another call on the radio. Mum got our message. Since she can't fly back to us, she got a cheap flight from O'Hare back to England. Somebody's renting our house, so she's going to stay with Sue and her mum, Mickey.

My mum has left me in this horrible place that is literally killing me and has gone home without me. How fair is that? When we moved it was evidently totally impossible for me to stay with Sue and Mickey so I could *do my exams in England.* But now it's fine for Mum to fly three thousand miles and stay there. What happened to all the "families stick together" stuff? I'll bet Mickey and Sue would both rather have me.

I take my sleeping bag and then hog the sofa, lying

with my face to the couch's back. I tell everyone to go away and leave me alone, and I fall asleep.

When I wake up again, it's dark. My body aches from lying on the sofa. I'm stiff and tense from the pain in my chest. I want to cough and I don't want to cough . . . if I cough, I know it's going to hurt.

So I just leave my body.

The windows are iced with frost. The cold pushes through two layers of glass and then under the thick door. It sneaks probing fingers through tiny chinks in the mortar between the logs and up through the felt and floorboards. If you lay your hand on top of the rug, you can feel where the cracks of the floorboards lie beneath the tightly woven wool. The cold is pushing through.

It pushes and pushes, all the time. It never sleeps.

In the room, people sleep. But not Jem, who sits by the woodburning stove. There is a ridiculously high pile of logs in the room; they spill from their brick niche. They climb the wall and sprawl across the floor.

Jem's shoulders are tense. He looks at the stove and at the logs and at me. Over and over he looks at the stove and then the logs and then at me. Then he notices Dad, who struggles in his sleep. Dad pushes against his sleeping bag, turning and muttering, still fighting in his war. Jem swallows as he watches and then looks at the stove. There is just room for another log.

He is already wearing the fireproof glove. The door

creaks open. He wedges the log on top of its burning fellows and creaks the door shut again.

The noise wakes Dad, who sits up, shaking a dream fight from his head. The young man and his father look at each other, across Tony's body, asleep, and mine, empty, as I watch from the rafters.

Dad jerks his head toward Jem's sleeping area.

Jem shakes his head, points to me.

Muttering, Dad picks his way over. I try to breathe deeply, like I'm asleep. Dad lays the back of his hand on my forehead and looks again at Jem. I'm okay, he says with his look. No fever.

Dad points sternly to Jem's bedding.

No. The shake of the head is final. Jem looks back me and the stove, as if Dad weren't even in the room.

Dad takes two steps and pulls Jem to his feet. Jem's huge now, but Dad lifts him as easily as if he were still a toddler. Dad pulls the fireproof glove from Jem's hand and tries to push him toward his bedding.

Jem refuses to move.

Quickly and silently, Dad grabs Jem's neck and pulls. He takes Jem's head in his big hands.

I don't know what he's going to do—hit him? Bite him? Dad's face is grim. Jem struggles, trying to pull away. Neither of them wants to wake me.

It is a desperate, silent battle. It looks very much like the dream fight Dad has every night—it is that tense and fearful.

Closer and closer, Dad drags Jem's head to his own, as if

he will head butt him or crack his son's skull in his powerful hands. Jem can't get away.

It's a kiss.

That was what Dad struggled to do—kiss his son on his forehead. A father's blessing—a benediction. Forgiveness for letting the fire go out. Understanding that Jem is trying to make it up to us. Dismissal back to his bed, to become a child again, not to keep trying to be a man before his time.

All of it, all of it. They understand each other better than anyone else could ever understand them. They can say everything with their eyes . . . or with a kiss.

It's strange seeing them like this, seeing them just with them.

Jem sinks to his knees. He holds the pads of his palms to his eyes and silently weeps in shame. Dad, his hand still on the nape of Jem's neck, looks away. He's giving him privacy, but being there, too.

I can't make Jem feel better. I can't do anything.

Chapter Five

It is easy to kill a sleeping bear. It is not so easy to find one.

A grizzly bear will wait to enter her sleeping den until a blizzard. Some scientists think the bear waits until she is desperate to escape the weather. Some scientists think the bear has learned to hide.

Many parts of a bear are valuable, but the main prize is the gall bladder. Bears' gall bladders are dried and ground to make bear bile, and bear bile is valuable medicine in the Far East. Wild bear bile is as valuable as gold.

* * *

On the sixth day I try not to wake up.

Everyone else is awake. I feel dirty and sad. I try, try to go back to sleep, but my bladder feels like it's going to explode. I go to use the nasty toilet that everyone can hear. I'll have to clean it again today. The big water bottle takes up a ton of room, and I feel clumsy pouring water in the tank so that I can flush.

I want a bath. I want my mum. And most of all, I just want to go home.

I can't help it. I start to cry a little. But I soon shut myself up. I blow my nose and pour a sink of cold water so that I can wash. My face still feels greasy afterward. I can't really see the mirror—it's too dark in here. The window is a bright white square, but the light that comes in is gray. I can't really tell if I'm getting spots.

I brush my dirty hair and braid it. I use a washcloth and do what bits I can reach—the smelliest parts of my body. I spray body mist until I start to cough and have to leave the little room.

They're waiting for me at the table.

"Wow," Tony says. "How do you manage to look so nice?" He pulls out my chair. "She even smells nice," he says. "How does she do it?"

"She sprays a bunch of chemicals all over herself," Dad says. And then he says to Jem, "Hey! You kicked me!"

Jem looks at me sheepishly. Dad has made pancakes

and bacon with maple syrup, and he's remembered to put the low-fat butter substitute and the light syrup next to my plate. Even though I'm supposed to be gaining weight, I don't like the taste of the real stuff anymore.

All three of them are looking at me as if I have to decide whether or not this is good enough. Whether or not we can keep on going.

When I smile, because I can't help it, they all relax. Boys are so simple—it makes them restful to be around. But it's kind of lonely to be with just boys.

I take a pancake and some bacon, and I listen to them debating what exercise I could take. And I suddenly get it; since they are stuck here without anything to do, I have become their project.

Apparently, I'm going to learn to shoot a rifle. We're going to shoe into the national forest, which is less than a half a mile away. Dad is going to radio the rangers, just in case they hear any shots. It's illegal to discharge a firearm in the park, but not in the national forest.

Nobody asks me. They look at me every once in a while, and nod a lot. But they don't actually speak to me.

I chew and swallow and chew and swallow. It seems like forever. And then I brush my teeth at the sink and sit on the sofa while they all scurry around, solving the problem of me.

Since I've been sick, nobody has come out walking with me. Mum was so busy catching up, and Dad and

Jem have been at work and school. I can tell they're all shocked by how slowly I shoe.

But actually, I'm going quite quickly, for me. I think I'm getting a little better. It's going to be a whole lot easier to get up the hill the next time I go see my bear.

Though I won't ever go again.

Because that was either stupid or insane.

The clearing is in the other direction. I shoe here sometimes, because I've seen hares and even elk come to look for the tall grass tops poking through the snow. But I've also seen wolves trotting through, and they scare me.

The targets are too far away when we stop. Dad says, "This is the place." He heaps up some snow and puts a tarp on the ground. He talks a long time about safety and recoil and how to use the sights, and he's so serious that it's kind of cute, so I try to listen.

We lie on our fronts to start shooting.

We have two rifles and two targets. Dad and Jem go first, and then they go and check their shots while Tony and I reload. We're pretty fast at this, after the time trials, and the sun feels warm on the dark green tarp. I am almost asleep again when they come back.

It hurts your shoulder worse than you can imagine, but shooting a rifle is also kind of fun. I get this illusion that I'm powerful and strong. I think I've hit the target almost every time. And then it's our turn to shoe down and look while Dad and Jem reload.

I have two holes, both on the left-hand edge of the targets. All of Tony's shots are drilled into the center.

I look at him, and he shrugs. "I used to be into it," he says.

He's only, what, sixteen or seventeen? Like Jem. I say, "When were you into it?"

He says, "When I was nine or ten." And then he says, "Stop looking at me like I'm some kind of freak."

And I say, "Sorry." And then: "But you are."

And something about that makes his eyes crinkle up on the corners. He looks at me, really looks at me, and he says, "Darcy . . ."

Dad shouts, "Hurry up!" So we peel off our papers and press down one each for Jem and Dad. Tony crumples his paper into a ball. When we get back Dad looks at mine and says, "You're pulling to the left."

I say, "No duh."

"How did you do?" he asks Tony.

Tony shrugs. "Okay."

The second time we lay back on the tarp, it's not warm anymore. Tony gets me to stand up off the snow. I'm starting to feel tired, and there's a wind coming up. Then Dad hurries over. He tells me and Tony to go back to the house. We get our shoes on and start off right away. Dad and Jem will catch up with us.

The oxygen seems to have fallen out of the air. The wind is pushing me down into the snow. The house isn't getting any closer, and the snow under our feet starts blowing up to our knees.

The boys look worried, and I try to hurry, but then I get that black spots thing again. I hurt everywhere.

I keep trying to leave my body, but I know that if I do, I'll fall down. I'm holding myself in.

Then Tony takes the rifle and the targets from Dad. It's all way too big for him to carry, but he manages. Jem takes the tarp, as well as his rifle and targets. Dad takes me. He puts me up over his shoulder, and we hurry. The sky is getting darker and lighter at the same time. The pressure of the air is hurting my head, which is bouncing all over the place because Dad is running.

We're late because of me. The storm is going to catch us out here, and it's my fault, because I'm too slow. And they all could get back perfectly safely, but they won't, because they won't leave me.

We're going to be caught out here in a blizzard, and it's my fault.

And I think, *I actually kind of like being out of my body. Why don't I just go ahead and die and save everybody else a lot of trouble?*

But then I think about Jem crying and how horrible it would be for Dad to pull me down off his back, all dead. So I stay in my body, and bounce.

When the snow starts it's like someone flicked a switch. It's suddenly everywhere at once. Tony starts shouting. He's found the porch. Dad shouts to put the targets and the tarp under the lashed-down canoe and carries me inside. Jem comes in with an armful of logs, and then Tony is trying to push the door shut, but the wind won't let him. He's leaning all his weight against it, and it's just pushing him back, and the snow and the wind are coming into the house, and the lamp goes out, and Dad has to go and help him.

And then suddenly, the moment the door shuts, it's all okay. We're back in, safe. I sit down at the table and half gasp, half laugh. We're all still wearing snowshoes.

After a cup of tea I get to my feet. I have some little black spots, but I want to clean the toilet. Everyone says that they'll do it, but I insist. And then, I lie down on the sofa again, with my back to everyone.

When I wake up, Dad brings me a bowl of beef stew and four crackers. We only had four crackers left. The boys have gone without so that I can have them all.

I eat the crackers first, using the stew like a dip. They all watch me, and I make little *num, num* sounds. They get happy about that. Project Darcy again.

Eating the stew takes forever. My arm feels heavy by the time I can put my spoon to rest in the bowl. Tony washes them both for me. Jem fills a water bottle. Dad has gone upstairs for a little table, and they put it by the sofa for my book and my own little lantern and some water. There is my duvet, too—from my bed, across my feet. It has pretty roses all over it. Dad says, "You can sleep there tonight. You don't have to move, unless you want to."

He's just now figured out how sick I am, now that there's no way of doing anything about it.

Tony comes and uses the sofa as a backrest. He's been washing his hair in the sink with cold water. I touch it, and it feels nice.

He says, "I'll wash yours for you, when it warms up a bit." He leans his head into my hand, and it reminds me of Mouser, our cat that died. She used to do that, used to lean in for caresses.

I say, "Tony?"

I don't have to. After all, he's only inches away. But I want to say his name.

And he says, "Yes?" and leans back a little bit more into my hand.

I say, "Tell me more stories about bears." But then I fall asleep like that, with my hand still tangled in his silky hair.

Chapter Six

It's over. I wake up because I'm hot. Someone has stripped off my duvet, but I'm hot anyway. It's very bright. I look out the window, and it's sunny, but it's more than that. There are lights on in the kitchen.

There's central heating.

The door to the stairs isn't taped shut anymore. There's a note on my little table. It says: "Breakfast is in the microwave. We're off to work/school. Jem will be back after three. The doctor is coming this morning. Do what he tells you. Love, Daddy."

I open the cupboard to carry up my boxes, but somebody already has. There's a sign on the washing machine door that says, "Please start me," in Jem's handwriting. But I wait to do that.

I take a bath. I shave my legs and wash my hair. I blow my hair dry and do my nails, and by then, I'm pretty hungry. I put on a fresh set of base layers and a rose-colored fleece. I put on matching rose-colored wool socks and lipstick. As much as I can, stuck in this place, I feel pretty.

The doctor comes while I am eating breakfast. He approves of the omelette and potatoes and shares some of my pot of tea.

He listens to my lungs, and frowns when he does. He thinks that days inside with woodburning stoves and oil lanterns in crowded conditions haven't done me any favors. He tells me he doesn't think I should go back to school for a couple more weeks. He talks to me more about the benefits of fresh air and how I need regular amounts of sunlight. He asks if I feel I could go out today for at least an hour.

No, I want to say. Getting clean, dressed, and fed is about enough for me today. I'm ready for a nice nap.

But I remember Dad's note, and nod. "Sure," I say. "I can do an hour."

The bear is swimming. Up, up, up; rising, buoyantly and irresistibly, in her consciousness. What wakes a bear? The sun has moved, and the inside of the cave is bathed in golden light. The icicles at the entrance, formed by her breath, are melting. Bear shifts off her bad shoulder. Her nose twitches.

* * *

I am still wearing the clashing lavender hat. At the bottom of the hill I hesitate, looking around, as if I am really being watched. But there is no one watching me but me.

I prod the snowpack with a pole. Again I hesitate.

And then, steadily, I begin the work of climbing the steep rise. The top has been scoured by the wind. The rock ledge is nearly clean of snow. I sit down and look for a view, but all I can see are trees.

And it hurts my head anyway, looking through my body eyes and my mind's eye at the same time.

In the sun I am quickly drowsy. I see my eyes pulling shut. I start to lie down on the warm rock, but the ledge is wet—the thin layer of snow has melted in the time it took to recover my breath. Behind me an icicle crashes.

And again, I am pulled to the cave.

I'm not thinking straight. I have the black spots, and I need to lie down. I duck into the cave because the cave is where I do that. I go because there is no place else for me to go.

It is the first time it's been light enough see her. She is massive. She is massive, and she has enormous claws. Her lips are slack, in her sleep, and I can see her huge, tearing teeth.

I suddenly feel a lot more energetic. I have to get out of here. This is utterly stupid. I will be killed in a horrible way, torn apart by an angry grizzly bear.

But then I see my hat. It's near her, but, thank goodness, she's not actually sleeping on it. It's snagged in the pine branches she's used for a mattress.

I think to myself one of those thoughts that you later realize is totally insane. I think, *I'll get my hat, and then I'll leave, and I'll never tell anybody. It will be like it never happened.*

I creep forward.

Again, the bear is cold where she should be warm. Where there should be fat, furry bodies sleeping against her. Again, she wakes to remember: the men took them. She chased. She caught one of their mules in a mighty swipe, cutting down through its haunch with her right foreclaws. And then the loud noise, and the fire in the bone of her shoulder.

She ran. She left her cubs and ran. Can a bear feel shame?

The bear shakes her head. She cries out and opens her eyes, comes unsteadily to her feet. One of the men is in her den.

Just as I reach for the bright red hat, the bear roars to her feet. I scrabble back, trip over my snowshoes, and end up crouching, my back to the wall of the cave.

The bear huffs. She rears up and slams her front paws inches from my feet. She roars in my face.

I see myself trembling violently. I am shouting something. I'm saying, "It's me, it's me." I clutch my hat to my heart, as if it will protect me. I look so small and weak.

Suddenly, the bear reaches out. She drags me forward.

I start to cry.

The bear sniffs at my head and neck. My eyes are shut tightly, and I whimper and shake. The bear nuzzles my chest, like a giant dog.

Still shaking, I see myself open my eyes and tentatively raise one hand to stroke the huge head. "It's me," I say again. "It's only me."

The bear snorts and swings away. Out on the ledge she urinates and defecates. On the other side, fastidiously, she eats some snow, and licks the water from what icicles she has not knocked down with her giant body.

Looking from out of my body, above, I can clearly see the dark patch of the bear's wounded shoulder.

The bear swings back into the cave and collapses heavily on her side. She opens her huge arms and makes an imperative call. And I, hesitantly, go to be embraced.

Chapter Seven

Her arm is heavy, and she smells. So do I. I wet my pants when she grabbed me. I only think, *I am in so much trouble. I am in so much trouble. I am in so much trouble.*

What if she won't let me go? But after about twenty minutes, she shifts a little bit, and I can edge away. I have to put my snowshoes back on properly to stand up. I think about the claws and how she could just casually rip my back from my bones. But she only gives a little snuffle at my place. I think she misses me when I am gone.

Then I am out on the ledge with her very smelly poo. And then I am going down the hill and I feel . . . I feel incredible. I feel like I could fly down. It seems easy to get to the bottom of the hill. It seems easy to shoe home.

When I'm back inside the cabin, I strip naked, push my stuff into the washer, and start it. I go up and take a shower. I keep laughing to myself, like a lunatic. I think I might be a lunatic. I really, really do. Maybe I've totally and utterly lost my mind.

After I'm dry and dressed, I look at what there is to make for dinner and decide to do some baking. I make two loaves of bread. While I am waiting for the dough to rise the first time, I make chocolate chip cookies. While I wait for the dough to rise the second time, I make cupcakes. I ice them in pastels when the bread goes into the oven. So I don't waste the heat I've made, I make a chicken casserole for dinner, too, and turn the oven down low.

It's not quite one o'clock. I'm clean, and everything is ready for tea. All of a sudden, I'm tired again. I get my laptop and plug it in. I lie on the sofa and watch a silly rom com; one of my DVDs from Sue.

I wonder if my mum will go see a movie at the multiplex. I wonder if she'll sleep in Sue's room, in the spare bed they always call "Darcy's bed." I wonder if she and Sue will hug goodnight, like me and Sue, and me and Mum, do.

I wonder if I'll ever forgive them.

* * *

Jem comes home in a whirl of news and movement. He dumps his stuff by the stairs and eats four chocolate chip cookies before I even manage to say hello.

He says, "Nancy's coming to clean in the morning," and eats another cookie. His skin is starting to turn into his summer color. It's spring now, and the bus has to come all the way to Mammoth to meet the park kids because they can't snowmobile into Gardner anymore.

He says, "I made the baseball team today. I got four hits and bowled . . ." He catches himself and shakes his head. His blond hair fans out like a mane. It needs cutting, I think, but then he shakes it back into place. "I mean, I *pitched* a bit, too. But there's all these rules about strike zones and things. . . . I don't know if I'll be able to do it."

He'll be able to do it. He'll probably have a trophy for it by summer. I just look at him, and he grins. "Oh, yeah," he says. "Mum is going to fly back the day after tomorrow."

I pour tea and then cut a cake, and Jem puts four more cookies back into the tin. He tells me that the first of the summer employees have arrived, and they are working, getting the hotels ready to open. He also says that dad's postgraduate helper is on her way, so Dad won't be so busy.

Then he says, "I've got tons of homework. Do you mind if I take my cake and tea upstairs?"

I'm exhausted just listening to him. I say, "No, you

go on," and wave him up the stairs. I get back on my sofa.

A rough paw is stroking my head. Even in my sleep, I know it's her. I lie perfectly still. I hardly breathe. If only she keeps her claws away from my skull. If only she lets me go.

But it's Dad, stroking my forehead with his rough hand.

He has news too. He's going to take me out on Saturday. First we are going to go to the bear awareness class that the park service holds for the summer employees, because I missed the one at school and have to have my bear awareness training. Then we are going into town for the night. Jem and Tony are going to stay in the cabin and do Dad's observations. Nancy is going to come and cook for them and do a really big cleaning. On Sunday morning we'll pick Mum up at the airport, as a surprise.

Jem eats almost a whole loaf of bread with his casserole and has seven cookies and then two more cupcakes for dessert. After dinner, Dad gives me my USB back. He has loaded on a bunch of pages about bears, so that I don't look stupid at the training event. There's also an email from Sue. I take it up to my room and sit on my bed to read everything.

Sue says she has loved having Mum there, but it makes her miss me even worse. She says she understands now how sick I was. She says she's not surprised

I got sick, and if it was her living here, she'd probably die in about five minutes.

It's very sweet and everything, but it's also irritating. They've all been talking about me.

I look at all the bear pages, flicking through. I know what grizzlies look like. I know how they hibernate. There's a bit about how they keep their cubs with them for two or three years. Something about that feels painful, and I think about my bear.

I know she is hurt, and I look to see what she should be doing this time of year, the beginning of spring. Eating meat. She should be eating an elk carcass or stealing a deer kill from a pack of wolves. She will be vegetarian for most of the summer, but she needs meat now.

How will she get some meat? I wonder if she's well enough to fight wolves. I wonder if she's well enough to leave the cave. I wonder if the meat she eats will be me.

Dad sticks his head in the doorway. "You okay?" he asks.

I nod, still thinking. He says, "I'm going to make some cocoa. Are you coming down?"

I say, "Yes, I'm absolutely fine," which we both know is not true. Dad nods like he believes me, but we both know he doesn't.

On the way down the stairs I say, "By the way, I found my hat."

* * *

On Friday I sleep late, again. When I get up Dad and Jem have already gone. Dad's note says "There's porridge in the microwave. Could you move the food on the porch into the freezer? We might get a bit of a thaw today. Love, Dad.

"Oh," he's written at the bottom. "And take pepper spray when you go out. The bears are waking up."

The porridge is all gloopy on top. I scrape it into the bin and make some blueberry muffins and microwave some bacon.

The oven and the microwave and the shower still all seem really wonderful. Like they were invented yesterday or something.

I decide I'd better move the freezer stuff first because I'll be too tired to do it when I get home. Dad's just stuffed it all into the animal-proof barrels, so I lay it out on the porch to try to organize it. He crumpled up all the boxes and torn some of the wrapping. It's a mess. I prop the door open and get some freezer bags, trying to save what I can.

Somebody gave us a whole deer last year, and I know that goes in the bottom of the freezer. Mum doesn't like the taste, and Dad is conflicted about it, he says. He told Tony to take some of it home, but Tony forgot.

It's not until I've already buried it in the freezer that I suddenly realize—I've got all this meat. . . .

Sunlight on a billion ice crystals. Without sunglasses it is blinding. It is also beautiful. Light dances through the air—refracted, reflected off innumerable crystal facets. The landscape glitters, like the idea of diamonds. People ski through a dream of diamonds.

There is a steady drip-drip. *Every so often the covering snow becomes too wet, too heavy, to lie on branches, and a cap of it crashes to the forest floor. I struggle with a heavy pack and my snowshoes and kick shut the door of the cabin. The entire snow sheet on the porch's roof creaks and thunders and slides. I am, for a moment, inside a wall of snow. Then it explodes at the bottom of the porch steps. I jump and curse.*

Shrugging into overalls and a coat, I leave the coat unzipped, the red hat shoved into my pocket. Briskly at first, I begin shoeing toward the hill.

Wet snow sticks to the shoes. I have to stop every six or seven yards and use my poles to free my treads. Twice I am almost hit by falling snow from the pines. I begin looking up as well as down. It's slow going.

I'm breathless by the time I reach the bottom of the hill. I look for tracks, bear droppings. There aren't any.

"Hey!" I shout. My voice echoes in the forest. Birds fly away. Little rustlings and squeakings stop. The silence that follows is shaming, somehow. "Hey," I shout again. "It's time to get up!"

The bear finally appears. She peers down and sniffs the air.

I go up ten or fifteen feet and anchor my poles in the snow. I call softly, "It's me."

The bear makes a keening, whining noise. She paces along the edge of the ledge.

"Come down," I say. "It's time to get up."

The bear extends her good arm down into the snowpack, but when she brings the arm with the hurt shoulder forward, she moans. For a moment it looks as though she will tumble headfirst down the steep slope, but she scrambles back and moans again, this time in frustration.

I continue climbing. Halfway up the hill I stop again to catch my breath. The bear peers over the edge and tentatively reaches to pat the snow with her good arm.

"You can't, can you?" I ask.

The bear snorts and growls, pacing along the ledge again.

I take a few more steps. I keep looking up at the bear. But she makes no more attempts to leave.

As my head is about to come level with the ledge, I hesitate again. The bear looks down and calls imperatively. Come here!

I swallow. I can see how I look when I force my fear down my throat.

"I'm coming," I say. I unhook my pack and slide it up. When I can see over the parapet, the bear has retreated to the cave. She sits up to groom her shoulder. I move cautiously forward.

"Does it hurt?" I ask. I crouch down onto my knees.

The bear lumbers forward and sniffs at my chest and throat.

My hand shakes as I pet the huge head.

"I have something for you," I say. Slowly, I edge back to my pack, and the bear resumes grooming her wound.

The venison is inside four plastic bags and tucked into an animal-proof food canister. I wasn't taking any chances. My hands shake as I undo it. I have to be quick. The moment the bear smells the meat . . .

As soon as I open the first bag, the bear's head comes up, sniffing. As quickly as I can, I spill the deer shoulder across the ground, almost to where the bear is sitting.

The bear noses the meat and then looks piercingly at me. I find myself explaining, "I thought you might need—"

That's the end of our conversation. The bear concentrates solely on her meal. I watch for a while, and then tidy the ledge. I kick the bear's excrement over the side and heap some fresh snow to where she drank before.

"Well," I say to the feeding bear, "I'll see you later."

I retrieve my pack and slide off the ledge, to begin the slow steps down. Once, I forget to clean the snow buildup from my shoes, and slide ten feet or so, nearly losing a pole.

Chapter Eight

I have no idea what I'm doing. But she can't get down.

I know I'm being stupid. I know I should be telling the rangers about her. But I don't know what they'll do. They'll probably shoot her.

Maybe she's just weak, because of her shoulder. If I feed her a bit, she might get strong enough to come down. And then that will be it. She'll go her way, and I'll go mine.

The thought makes something catch at the back of my throat. For a second I don't know whether I'm going to cough, or cry, or just stop breathing forever.

But then I'm okay and thinking about making salmon fish cakes for dinner. And rice. Bears like fish, don't they? Maybe I could save her some.

I have no idea what I'm doing.

Can grizzly bears feel gratitude? Why should they? They live alone most of their lives. When they are together they seem like very young toddlers; aware of one another but with no intention of interacting. They will often fight over food or over a special place. Their mothers tenderly care for them, and it certainly seems the cubs and mothers love one another dearly. But once the cubs are grown, they may never see their mothers again. Worse still, they may not recognize them if they do.

To whom would a bear feel grateful?

I am almost all the way back to the cabin when suddenly, I can't move. I immediately have black spots, and my head hurts.

I drag a step and then another. The snow is building up on my snowshoes, but I just can't get it off. My arms are too weak to push it away with my poles. Now I have to raise my feet higher and higher to take each step, and it's slippery.

I don't know how I get to the porch. But we have a canoe stored there and I sit down on it, leaning on my pack against the wall. My poles drop from my hand, and I sleep in the warmth of the dancing sunlight.

I don't even hear the snowmobile. I just feel Jem shaking my arm and calling my name.

I open my eyes. I say, "Oh, hell. The fish cakes," and try to get up. Jem pushes me back down.

"How far did you go?" he asks.

"Just up that hill, where the path forks. Not far."

He is kneeling down, taking off my snowshoes.

"You've got the wrong shoes on. These are for powder." He looks up at me. "You must be totally whacked."

I rub my eyes. "I'm okay now," I say. Jem pulls my hands down and looks at my fleece gloves.

"You've got fur all over your gloves."

I'm suddenly aware that I've got a big pack on my back, with a food canister full of bloody plastic bags inside it. I say, "Could you get me a drink of water?"

And while he's gone I shrug off the backpack and push it under the canoe. There's an awful lot of stuff under that canoe. I have to push hard.

I take off my gloves and put them in my lap. I don't want him looking for them, thinking I'm hiding something. Though I am, of course.

"There's fur on your coat too."

I make a big deal out of drinking my water. I hand him the glass and then purposefully stagger a bit when I stand up. He's quick to grab me.

"Everything smells," I complain as we go inside. "Can you put my coat and stuff in the washer for me?"

He looks at my gear when he shoves it in. "You've got fur on your overalls as well."

I'm on the sofa. I say, "I'm sorry, is it a problem? Do you want me to do it?"

"No," he says. "I just wondered where you picked up all the fur."

I stand up. I say, "I made some blueberry muffins. I'll put the kettle on for tea."

Just like I knew he would, he says, "No, I'll do it. You sit down."

And the subject is dropped.

The fish cakes turn out well, and I sneak half a salmon into the food canister in my pack under the canoe. I'll add some frozen venison in the morning, and that ought to keep her going over the weekend.

Dad goes on and on about the snowshoes. He talks to me like I'm an idiot. I read somewhere that the Inuit have something like forty words for "snow." Well, my dad has a snowshoe solution for every single one of them. Boring is not the word.

We all go up to bed after the dishes are done. Dad wants to get an early start, and Jem has baseball practice in the morning. I wash and brush and get into bed. Bed still feels like the best place on earth. I am reading a book I've read before and love. I feel cozy and warm and nice.

Dad and Jem come to say goodnight. They stand

in my doorway, stripped down to their base layers and socks. Dad says, "What's all this about being covered in fur? What *did* you get up to today?"

I say, without looking up, "Oh, you know, I was hugging a grizzly bear."

Dad says, "Ha-ha," and kisses me goodnight.

Jem rolls his eyes. He says, "Goodnight, stupid," and shuts my door.

I feel very clever, and I want to tell Sue all about it so badly that I reach under my pillow for my phone. It's a reflex. But my phone is at the bottom of my underwear drawer, not even charged. And Sue wouldn't understand anyway.

Dad is still home when I come downstairs the next morning. He is putting bolts into the logs of the cabin, so that I can hang my outdoors clothes on carabiners to air. He has his climbing gear out on the table.

"We've got to be careful about water usage," he says. I think I'm supposed to feel guilty about washing my overalls and coat so much. But I don't. He knows I don't, so he adds, "And anyway, we're not making much money on this project. They're not meant to be washed every day." Okay, so now I feel a bit guilty. I must look guilty anyway, because he shuts up about the great crime of me washing my clothes.

I pick up a little metal pulley and start thinking.

I've done my share of rock climbing. In our family that means I've done a lot. I've used most of the stuff in the climbing bag, but I haven't ever set a bolt. If we're climbing someplace that doesn't already have climbing routes, Dad puts bolts in the rock, so that we can hook the ropes to them and not fall to our deaths if one of us does something stupid.

I follow Dad out to the porch and watch from my seat on the canoe. I ask all kinds of questions about how you go about placing bolts into rock, and he seems really happy to answer. He shows me special glue and stuff and goes into great detail about flaky rock and hard rock and drilling angles.

Then he looks at his watch and gets all worried because he's running late. I say that I'll put the stuff away, so that he can take off sooner, and he thanks me.

I feel a little guilty again about fooling him. But it doesn't last long.

I have a lot to do today. I have to pack for town. I can wear real shoes, jeans, a dress and tights. . . . I can wear a wool jacket, my cashmere cardigan. But I haven't seen a fashion magazine for months, and I don't want to look like a goof. I also don't want to look all classic and buttoned-up and preppy. It's tricky.

I play music, loud, with the door to the porch propped open. The singer's voice warbles with emotion.

Not far away, a pack of wolves warbles back.

I might have been playing music a little loud. I don't even hear the snowmobile. I've got a ton of meat and some climbing gear in my pack, which is just sitting there, by the open door, where anyone can see me taking it all out into the forest.

Then this huge stranger just walks into my house unannounced. He's covered in black and wearing dark sunglasses. He looks like every hit man in any movie you ever saw. My heart races as I fumble with the remote control for the stereo and turn it off.

Then he takes off sunglasses, and I see it's a woman. It's Nancy, who is going to help with cleaning. She's just pretty big.

She smiles. "Guess you're a teenager, all right," she says. "My daughter used to love to blast it."

Wolves are howling, not too far away.

Nancy laughs. "You got them going. They musta liked it." She kicks off her boots and steps inside. "I'm more of a country-and-western girl myself."

I make her a cup of tea, and Nancy talks to me about what needs doing and what she should cook for tonight and for the boys over the weekend. I show her what's left in the freezer and the store cupboard and the fridge. I think there's still tons of food, but she says, "I'd say it's about time Marcus got his butt into town to stock up." She likes my menu ideas. "You're real creative."

I feel like I should stay and help, but Nancy pushes

me out the door. "If Doc Hudson told you to get fresh air, you'd better go and get it. Marcus says you get real tired in the afternoons."

I sit down on the canoe and put on the wet-weather snowshoes. I wish she'd go start doing things, but instead she watches me. "That's right," she says. "Under there. That's right," as if she's in charge of me getting my shoes on.

And then there's nothing for it. I pick up the pack, and I can't help but huff a little, getting it on my back. It's so heavy.

"What's in there?" Nancy asks, just like I was afraid she would.

"I'm trying to build up my wind."

She nods, like carrying a bunch of rocks on my back would be a sensible thing to do. "That doctor. Some people think he's got funny ideas. But we think the world of him up here."

That's because you're all gung-ho, outdoor nutcases like Dad and the kids at school, I think.

And finally, finally, after watching me shoe into the trees, she shuts the door of the cabin.

This pack weighs a million pounds. Thank goodness I have on the right shoes. Dad and Jem know what they're talking about. It's a whole lot easier, and the WD-40 they sprayed on the bottoms works really well. It's almost like walking.

A bear paces the ledge. Back and forth, back and forth.

The swing of her torso is impossibly heavy. She is astonishingly graceful. Every movement shows her power.

And then, her shoulder catches, seizes somehow. It's horrible to see; like a slashed painting. Something beautiful is destroyed when she limps and staggers.

She complains vigorously, nose in the air, moaning. Shakes her shaggy head.

And continues pacing, with the remains of her ursine grace.

"Hey," I call. "Hey."

The bear peers down. Roars her impatience.

"All right, keep your fur on."

Now the ledge extends, snow free, down over two feet. I watch myself look at it. What I thought was a hill is really a cliff face. I'll never get up here when the snow is gone.

I begin climbing the wet, slippery snow. It makes neat stairs, though my poles are sinking deeply into it. I see myself wavering back and forth and know it is a struggle to keep from falling.

The bear is alternately shouting and calling.

Toward the top, I lose my patience and shriek at her.

Her face peers down at me over the edge, quizzical. I watch myself shake my head.

"I'm doing my best!" I shout, and then say it nicely. "I'm doing my best." I hurt everywhere.

I give her the food and kick all her poo off the edge and try to tidy up as much as I can.

When I leave she is trying to eat the frozen deer carcass. I get all the way down to the ground before she remembers me and looks down over the edge of the cliff.

She looks down and kind of whimpers. I guess she wanted a hug.

Chapter Nine

Nancy is gone when I get back, and I go straight upstairs to pack, after anchoring my overalls and my coat on the carabiner. Although I don't need to, because I didn't cuddle the bear. I didn't know she wanted a cuddle. I thought she only wanted food. I guess she wants both.

I have no idea what I'm doing.

The thing with the bear has really rattled me, and I nearly pack slim-legged jeans and loafers, when I know the loafers and jeans look dreadful with socks, and I also know it won't be warm enough to go without them.

My mind is all over the place.

She looked sicker than she did before. She's not getting better. She's getting worse. Being awake isn't helping her.

And I'm not sure I'm feeding her enough.

I have no idea what I'm doing.

I take all my clothes out of the bag and start again. Jeans. Leather boots. Denim skirt. Blue wool coat. Hot pink cashmere. White T-shirts. Stripy scarf. Rosebud earrings. Pajamas, washbag, makeup. Done, done, and done. That wasn't hard, was it?

All the bending and lifting finishes me off. I can't even be bothered to clean the other clothes off the bed. I curl up around them and sleep.

"Hey, Sleeping Beauty." Jem is in the doorway, with Tony, and they are laughing at me curled around my neatly piled clothes.

"I've made a pot of tea, and Nancy has made some iced buns."

Tony smiles at me, his lazy, sweet smile that makes my heart thump in my chest. "Cinnamon rolls," he corrects Jem. "They're called cinnamon rolls."

I could listen to Tony Infante say "cinnamon rolls" all day long. I'm sure I blush.

We go downstairs. Tony has printed out a list of what movies are showing in Bozeman, and we read them and argue about what I should see. When Dad comes back the dinner is beef bourguignonne, and Nancy has made crepes that we microwave. Guess she's a bit creative herself. Dad gets out a bottle of wine, and we are all allowed a little glassful.

Evidently, Mammoth's Park Service Office is being funny about taking in packages right now, and Tony wants a new pair of Vans—special skateboarding shoes. He can't order them, so he gives me a little piece of paper with style numbers and sizes. If I can, I'm to get the ones at the top, but if not, the next and the next, and so on.

We're sitting at the table, and his head is bent over the list as he's explaining it to me, but I totally get it already. My head's bent over the list too, just to show him I'm taking it seriously. When he looks up, his nose is only about two inches away from mine, and he looks into my eyes, and my stomach does this dropping away thing.

Jem clears his throat. "You didn't ask what I want."

Tony is still looking at me. I've looked away, but I can feel his eyes on my face. I say to Jem, "I know what you want. You want all your favorite junk food."

Dad groans. "Not those cheesy things. They smell like a urinal."

But even though I'm pretending to interact with my family, really, I'm in another world, and it's a world where only Tony Infante and I exist. I slide my hand a half an inch closer to his, and he slides his hand a half an inch closer to mine.

"I don't care what they smell like," Jem says. "And anyway, you can talk. I'll bet you bring back beef jerky."

And then we are touching hands, me and Tony. And he pushes, just a little, with his hand on mine, and I push, just a little back.

And I think I might die from it. My heart is beating so hard that I'm finding it hard to breathe, and I'm starting to get a few black spots.

I pull away and lean back in my chair. Tony keeps looking down at his list, as if he's studying it, but his lips curl into a secret smile. . . . I've got to stop looking at Tony Infante's lips. . . . I'm going to pass out right here at the table.

Then Tony puts the list into an envelope full of money and hands it to me.

And just for a moment, I stop thinking about how completely gorgeous Tony Infante is, and think.

Money.

Mum and Dad have been giving me twenty-five dollars a week, and I've just been throwing it into a drawer.

I run up the stairs and nearly faint on the landing. But even though I've got big black spots, I still find my room and the drawer. I bring the money down, using my fleece like a basket.

Tony and Jem count it while I pant at the table. I have almost six hundred dollars. Dad says I can treat *him* to a movie, and he'll see anything I want.

What does a bear know about death? The bear has seen many animals die. She has killed thousands of animals to feed herself: young elk, fish, even moths. She has seen other bears die.

But does she know that *she* will die? Does she even think of herself as a separate being? She perceives the world with her consciousness, but how aware is she that her consciousness forms her perceptions? Does she know those perceptions are embodied in a frail husk of degrading cells? Is she aware enough of others to think that the world might go on without her?

No one knows if a bear fears death. It might be only the pain and the hunger that make her cry, in the den that is now her prison.

Jem and Tony drop us off on the snowmobiles, and Dad and I walk about a mile with our packs. It's like walking into spring. Behind us is land still locked in snow. Here, there are little flowers pushing up. The birds are going crazy. Grass and flowers and birds and being able to walk on the ground. It's all amazing. It's so much easier than shoeing that it hardly hurts me at all.

My class is right in the tourist center. I walk in, and everyone turns and looks at me.

I haven't seen other people for months, and now I have about a hundred of them staring at me. They're all wearing ordinary clothes: dresses and jeans and T-shirts and striped cotton sweaters. I'm wearing head-to-toe Gore-Tex. I slide my pack down by the wall and push my sunglasses up on top of my head. I try to look normal and give a little smile. And they start talking to one another again.

The ranger at the front looks kind of familiar. He waves at me, and I wave back. And then he waves again, and I can tell he's calling me forward. He's saved a seat for me in front. He's put his hat on it.

So I have to walk down the aisle in front of all these people and hand the ranger his Smokey the Bear hat and sit down. I'm sure my face matches the red patches on my coat by the time I do. He leans over and says, "You probably know most of this already. It's just a formality."

The doctor told me that being nervous can make my breathing worse. I notice, now that I'm sitting down, that I'm wheezing a bit.

This girl sitting next to me has bright bleached hair and a nose ring. She smiles and says, "Asthma?"

Not "Hi." Not "My name is Whatever." Just "Asthma?"

I blush again. I hate myself for blushing, and I hate her for having no manners. I shake my head. I say, "I'm all right."

She puts out her hand and says, "I'm Marcie." And suddenly, I realize she's got quite nice manners.

I shake it and say, "Darcy."

"We rhyme!" She laughs. "Where are you working?"

"I'm not," I say. "I live here. My dad works here."

"Oh, wow!" she says. "You lucky thing. All year?"

I nod. She tells the guy on the other side of her. Now everybody in the front row is leaning to listen to our conversation.

"What does your dad do?"

"Is that your dad?" the guy asks, pointing to the ranger in front.

The girl on the other side of me says, "Have you ever seen a bear?"

"Have you seen wolves?"

"How deep was the snow?"

It's like being a celebrity or something. Luckily, the ranger clears his throat, and somebody dims the lights for a PowerPoint presentation, so I don't have to answer.

I am so hot and embarrassed that I have to take off my coat. I miss the first slide.

The second slide is a picture. Black bear, brown bear.

The ranger says, "The easiest way to tell these two apart is by looks and behavior. The brown bear, which we call a grizzly, has a distinctive hump and is larger than the black bear."

New slide. Black bear.

"If you see a bear in the woods, and you run and climb a tree, and the bear climbs after you and kills you and eats you, that's a black bear."

Nervous laughter. New slide. Brown bear.

"If you see a bear in the woods, and you run and climb a tree, and the bear pushes the tree over and kills you and eats you, that's a grizzly."

Utter silence.

Well, he's got their attention. Now he goes on to talk about the unpredictability of bears, how few maulings there are per year, and how to keep yourself safe.

He talks about respecting bear closure signs on trails, staying at least a hundred feet from bears at all times, and reporting any aggressive bear behavior.

Then he talks about poachers. He shows a picture of some poor black bear with a dirty tube stuck in its stomach, and talks about bear farming. He shows pictures of dead bears with their paws cut off, and talks about how much bear paws are worth in the Far East. Some of the girls start to cry. He tells us how to be alert for poaching.

That's what happened to my bear, I think. They tried to get her, but she got away. Or maybe she went over into the national forest, and some city person shot her, thinking she was an elk.

When I pay attention again, the ranger is talking about the bears waking up. He tells us about how they eat winterkills or steal kills from wolf packs. He tells us how much meat they need their first few weeks of coming out of hibernation.

It's a lot more than what I've already given her.

Hunger is an injustice. It is insulting. It burns in your belly and knocks on all the doors of your mind. Of course, you are weak and tired, but you are also unhappy. The universe has decided you are not worth keeping. It will not waste any more of its resources on you.

When you are hungry you must conserve all energy that does not lead to nutrition. But your entire digestive system rumbles and cramps. Your digestive fluid burns. With nothing else to consume, it seems to decide to consume its host. Comfort is impossible.

You must rest, but you can't rest. You must keep positive and think creatively about how you will find food, but you are deeply, biologically, unhappy.

When you are hungry you feel trapped.

The bear sleeps whenever she can.

I am half asleep in the car. Images chase my dreaming mind. My friends, around a table at Pizza Hut, only it's not Pizza Hut, because they're all eating bear paws. Outside, screaming bears crowd the plate-glass windows, but I am the only one who can see them, who can hear them cry.

My bear, hungry, shoulder getting worse. Looking for me, waiting for me.

Three dirty men, leading ugly horses. They take my babies. My lovely, funny, round, and furry babies. The babies cry. I charge them. The men have dogs that bite at me. The men put cloth over my babies' faces, and my babies fall down. I am bitten on my throat. There is a dog on my back, too. I swing and roll.

The men are taking my babies away, on the ugly horses. I run after them. I swipe at the rump of a horse. It screams.

And then I am falling. A hammer blow. A burning. The sound, the smoke. Shot. I was shot in the shoulder. I hide in the brush. I let . . . I let the men take my babies away. This crushes my heart.

The bear with the dirty tube in its stomach. The bear in the cage. It's mine. It's my baby.

It's my baby. It's my baby. It's my baby.

"Darcy!" Dad is shaking me.

I am sweating and panting.

"You were having a nightmare."

I say, "God."

Dad offers me a bottle of water, and I gulp about half of it.

"What was it about?"

I drink a little more, just for time to think of what to tell him. Then I say, "Bears."

"I've heard some of those slides are pretty graphic. You okay?"

I nod. "Fine."

We're coming into Livingston. It's a pretty town, but it looks absolutely gorgeous to me. Dad asks, "Hungry? How does a burger and a shake sound?"

"It sounds like absolute heaven," I say. I'm going to enjoy every minute of this weekend. No matter what.

Whenever Dad gets a burger and they say, "Would you like fries or a salad?," he always says, "Both." Today they say, "Would you like coleslaw or fries?," and we both say, "Both, and can I have a salad, as well?" It's been so long since I've had fresh vegetables. The salad tastes amazing, and I get my favorite blue cheese dressing with full fat. Everything tastes so, so good. In the cabin I'm always conscious that I have to chew and swallow. But in the restaurant I just look up for a moment, and my food is all gone.

I feel like a python that's swallowed a rabbit whole.

We waddle back to the car, and there's a jewelry shop. I kind of linger, looking in the window, and Dad says, "Why don't you go in and look around? We're not in any tearing hurry."

And that's when I see it. It's a silver ring—heavy, thick, and shaped around the finger like a slightly irregular octagon. Every side has something on it—the carved silhouette of a grizzly, a bear's paw print with a Montana sapphire set into the palm, a pine tree, a mountain range, a tiny bear claw—inset and enameled. It's the most beautiful thing I've ever seen.

Before I know it I'm asking to try it on, and it fits. It's a little hard to slide over my knuckle, but once the ring is past, it fits perfectly.

Not only does it fit, but it's comfortable. It's also handmade, by an artist, and five hundred and forty-five dollars.

I was going to get a haircut. I was going to buy clothes. I was going to buy books.

I have the money, but I can't afford the ring. Not really.

Dad looks at me and then at the ring. He asks the guy if there's any discount for locals. He tells the guy that he's an ungulates researcher and stationed outside at an observation hut in Cooke City.

The guy goes back and talks to a lady.

They tell Dad they could knock off 20 percent.

Dad, very kindly, tells me that makes it four hundred and thirty-six dollars. He knows how bad I am at math.

I could run away with that much money. I could fly home myself.

The silhouette of the grizzly looks just like her. Somebody who has really looked at bears properly has made that ring. Someone who knows what they mean.

I hear my voice say, "I'll take it."

Dad gives me fifty dollars. He said, "I was going to buy you a present, for being such a trouper. But I'd really like to help you pay for that. It's beautiful."

We check into our motel, and bounce on the beds. We take really long showers. We change into actual clothes. Even Dad puts on a pair of cords and a cotton shirt with buttons. We wash the car. We go to a silly movie and eat candy and drink huge Cokes. I missed an exciting bit, running to the ladies' room.

Dad is a pretty fun date. I don't even mind when we go to a climbing store for, like, hours.

He's gotten us dinner reservations at a restaurant in a little yellow house. It has great Mexican food. At the end of our meal, he asks me how I'm feeling.

I'm absolutely stuffed, again. They kept bringing us chips and salsa, and I think I ate my body weight. But I feel fine.

"Not tired?" Dad asks.

I look at my watch. It's eight o'clock. In the park that's usually bedtime for me. "No," I say, "not tired."

We walk to the car, and Dad opens this bag on the backseat. He hands me my yellow bikini and a towel.

"We're going swimming," he says. He starts driving. We go clear out of town. I hope he's not taking me hot potting in one of those thermal places in the woods where you have to drop your clothes in the mud and get naked in front of everybody. But then we pull up into an actual parking lot at an actual building. Dad pays for us to go in and then points to the ladies' changing area.

It's below freezing tonight, but the changing room is warm. The air, when I come out, though, is cold and wet. Dad's already in the pool. "Come in quick!" he says. "It's really warm."

And it is. It smells a bit like boiled eggs, because it's thermal water—water heated by the depths of the earth. But it's lovely and warm.

For a moment I just float on my back. There's only about twenty people there and most of them are clustered at the edge, drinking beer and chatting. I start to swim. I go through all my strokes: front crawl, back crawl, breaststroke, butterfly. I dive under the water and pinch Dad's bottom when he's not looking. I do handstands and flips.

I shout, "I love this place!" Dad smiles, but he's looking at me kind of funny, too.

Suddenly, I remember my ring, and I panic a little bit, but it's still on nice and tight.

The moon is a sliver of ice in the cold sky. I wonder what the doctor would think of me getting wet like this. I don't care.

When we get back to the motel, Dad takes a shower first. I'm on my phone, updating my status: "Taking a break from the wilderness in an actual town. So cool to have concrete under my feet!" and texting Sue and my mates, BACK IN CIVLSATN FOR NIGHT. I tell them about the movie I saw and the food I ate. I take a picture of my new ring and post it.

Dad goes to sleep. I take a shower myself and come back and turn out the lights. Thirty-seven people like my status. The gang is sleeping over at Izzy's. They've been up all night at a party. They send me video of them in their pajamas, squealing and waving and blowing me kisses. They send me one of Izzy with a boy from the local private school, and I text her and ask her if she snogged him. She texts me back and tells me I'm just jealous 'cause all I can snog are moose. We copy everybody into our text, and there's lots of LOLs.

Then they send me a video of them all dancing at the party, and I get up and dance along.

Dad tells me to either put in my earbuds or shut it down—he's exhausted.

I put in my earbuds and keep dancing. I look at the window at the snow-capped mountains and describe it to the girls, telling them I'm dancing in the motel, that I'm dancing with them, and that they're dancing with me and the moon and the mountains.

I post photos I took ages ago of the cabin and the snowmobiles and skis and stuff. I tell everybody we've still got a three-foot snowpack.

People go crazy over the photos. Sue tells me I look beautiful and that she's going to start growing her hair out tomorrow.

People are asking me all about how we get food and stuff and if I have seen any wolves or bears. I post a Google Earth link showing where the cabin is. I post a link to the place we went swimming and talk about how amazing it was.

More people ask me questions. People from my old

school are following me like crazy, just to ask me questions.

I answer and answer, way past midnight, and fall asleep with my phone in my hand, plugged into the charger.

Chapter Ten

I don't really understand that something about me is strange until I wake up earlier than Dad.

I *never* wake up earlier than Dad. Dad wakes up earlier than everybody. Every single day. He's usually already had a three-mile run by the time my alarm goes off.

I look at him, and he's still really out of it. So I get dressed in the bathroom and brush my hair into a ponytail and get the key and my bag and quietly let myself out. I walk down the street until I see a coffee place, and I get us bagels and cream cheese. I get Dad a large latte and me some English Breakfast tea with milk. They put it all into a paper bag with handles that makes it easy to carry, so I buy a paper, too. I take it all back to the room.

Dad's just sitting up, rubbing his face, and I give him his coffee, his paper, and his bagel.

"Oh, man," he keeps saying. "Oh, wow." Like I've just gone out and killed an elk, field dressed it, and cooked it over an open fire that I started with by rubbing two sticks together. If he gets that excited because I managed to buy bagels, he must think I'm totally useless.

So, I get back on my phone and pick up where I left off. Izzy has decided she hates that boy. Martha rather fancies him, though. Izzy says all he could do was talk about music. Martha says she likes music.

Sue posts another picture of the boy and Izzy, and Izzy goes mental and demands she takes it down.

I feel kind of sorry for Izzy. I tell everybody to leave her alone or I'll send a bear after them. Sue tells me in a private message that Izzy really needs to think more about how easily she talks to boys. Izzy gave that boy her phone number, and he sent her a disgusting picture. Sue posted the picture of Izzy cuddling him, so that she'll think more when she goes to the next party and not give out her number to total strangers.

I ask Sue if Izzy snogged the boy, and she says she doesn't think so.

I ask Sue if she's snogged anybody yet, and she says not really. She asks me if there are any boys here.

I think about Tony, about how he touched my hand and the feel of his silky black hair. I say not really.

* * *

Dad is standing by the bed, dressed. He says, "Do you want to rest up here for the morning?"

I say, "Don't be stupid. I want to go shopping." I'm packed in about five seconds.

We get Tony's shoes first, in case they don't have his size or something and we have to hunt. But they have his first pick in his size, and we're really pleased. Then we decide we need to do our other duty, and we hit the supermarket.

It takes us more than an hour to get everything on our list, and I get quite a bit that wasn't on it, as well, mostly for Jem. I tell Dad I have to get some stuff for Tony's family, and also buy a big box of cantaloupes, a huge sack of apples, and another huge sack of carrots. We pack it all into the back of the car. I'll have to ride with Mum's suitcase on my lap after we pick her up.

Then we go to a big box store and stock up on toiletries. I have enough money left for some new underwear and some of the faded cowgirl jeans everybody up here seems to wear. I change into them after I pay, and they look good with my boots, but Dad says I'll have to save up for some real cowboy boots. We go to a sushi bar for lunch, and drink a lot of homemade iced green tea. Next door is a place with Native American earrings, and I get some little silver feathers with tiny turquoise chips for me; Mum; Sue; and her mum, Mickey.

"Do you want to go back to the car?" Dad asks.

I look at my watch. "No," I say. "We've still got two hours till Mum's due to arrive."

"How much money have you got left?"

I count. Nearly fifty bucks. Dad says he owes me for this week's allowance, too. We're right outside a Western wear store. He nods at some boots in the window.

My father has *never* willingly gone shoe shopping with me before.

Five minutes later, we're back outside.

Dad is shaking his head. "Three hundred and eighty dollars!" he keeps saying. "Three hundred and eighty dollars!"

I say, "There were some cheaper ones."

"But they were crappy." He shrugs. "And they were still more than two hundred bucks."

"I know."

He looks at me again. He says, "Tired?"

No. And now even I realize that's a bit weird. We look at each other for a minute. "Maybe I'm all better?"

"You look great," he says. "Rosy and healthy and everything."

Now it's my turn to shrug. "I feel fine."

"And you didn't throw a fit about the boots."

I say, "I'm not two, Dad."

He says, "No, but you haven't been very . . . resilient . . . since we got here. The least little thing seems to make you angry."

I say, "Thanks." We walk a few steps. I say, "I'm surprised you've been around enough to notice."

He says, "I'm going to pretend I didn't hear that."

We look at this cool place with quilts, and I buy some greeting cards and a kit to quilt my own pretty pillow. We get a cup of tea and have a brownie. And then it's time to drive to the airport.

I'm not mad at my mum anymore. And I'm so glad to see her. She comes through, and she's just looking around to see where the bus goes from, squinting because she's got her glasses up on top of her hair and can't see the signs. And then she sees us and breaks into her lopsided smile with too much of her gums showing. She hardly looks at Dad. She's so glad to see me that she hugs me, over and over again, and keeps telling me how good I look.

We get into the car, and Dad starts driving back to the park. I text my friends until we're out of coverage. And then I just turn off my phone. I might be able to get a few more minutes at Mammoth, but I might not, and it will just make me sad if I can't.

Mum can't wait to get back to the park. She's all excited and asks us about a hundred questions. What did we buy for food? What did we have left? How did we manage during the storm? We blow through Livingston, and I look at my ring, my lovely, lovely ring.

The nearer we get to the park, the more ill I start to feel. At Mammoth, Dad talks to the rangers, and one of them comes out with his jeep. We load up all the groceries and toiletries into the jeep. He's going to drive us to our rendezvous spot with Jem and Tony. Dad parks the car and gets on the radio. After a whole lot about the observations, Dad reminds Jem to bring both sleds.

Mum rides with the ranger, because she's been traveling for so long. I have to walk, with my pack on my back. I take about five steps before I start to feel sick.

I can't breathe, that's the problem. Maybe I ate too much. I stagger along behind Dad, who keeps telling me to keep up. In no time I've got that pressurey feeling in my head. But no black spots. Not yet, anyway.

By the time we get to the rendezvous spot, I want to lie down and sleep in the snow.

Dad keeps telling me to help. He keeps saying I need to wake up and get with the program. I'm just stumbling around with boxes in my arms. I don't know what I'm doing.

Finally, Jem takes Dad aside, and they look at me. I hear Dad say, "But she was fine all weekend. She was running around like anything."

Jem says, "And now look at her. You've worn her out."

"No," Dad says, "Really. She was okay."

Jem comes over and makes me sit down on the snowmobile to rest. "Well, she's not okay now."

When we take off, Tony drives, and I snuggle behind him and lean back against Jem. I can hear Mum and Dad arguing in front of us as they start away. Arguing about me.

Then they stop, and Tony doesn't know that they're stopping so that they can be alone to argue, so he stops too.

I hear Dad say, "No, I don't want to believe the worst about her. But what can I think? When she's getting her own way, she's fine!"

Tony suddenly gets the fact that they're fighting and hits the throttle. Jem gives me a cuddle. He shouts "It's not true!" in my ear.

We rumble along, but I wonder. Is Dad right? Do I deliberately get tired because I hate this place?

I feel under my glove where my ring is cold against my finger.

But I don't hate it. I don't.

When we get in I manage to get Tony to one side and tell him to put the melons and the carrots and the apples under the canoe. I tell him to pretend they're for him. I tell him I'll explain later.

But I hope I won't have to.

He loves his shoes. And I got him a matching key ring, too. I tell him it's for being so helpful during the storm, but that's just because everyone else is listening. He holds it really tightly in his hand, and his eyes shine when he thanks me.

Dad pays him some actual cash for helping with the observations and then gets him to take some of the venison. Dad thinks that Nancy fed a bunch of venison to the boys while we were gone. He keeps saying they must have eaten like kings.

Jem can't believe I've remembered all his favorite junk food. I got him about twenty frozen Hawaiian pizzas, and a whole bunch of Cheetos, and all his favorite American candy, including all the spicy Jolly Ranchers. And some Clearasil, because he gets really spotty if he eats junk.

I give Mum her earrings.

Now that all that is settled, I sit down on the sofa. In two minutes I'm asleep.

I wake up. It's the middle of the night, and Dad is watching me. He says, "Do you want to go to bed?" When I say yes, he carries me up, like I'm little again. He waits for me to use the bathroom, and then he helps me out of my clothes and tucks me in.

He says, "Either you're . . . I don't know . . . a horrible teenage monster . . . or there's something weird going on."

I am too tired to answer. I just look at him and go back to sleep.

When I get up, there's nobody home. Even Mum has gone out. The note says, "I have to check my email. I'll snowmobile to the melt line and be back soon. XX Mummy."

And I think, *Good. I can feed my bear.*

I use the sled.

I take a big plastic storage box, the rest of the venison, the cantaloupes, the carrots, and the apples. I take all the climbing stuff I think I'll need, too. I've got a plan for dealing with the cliff.

On my way up, I scrape the snow back and set three bolts. I can't believe how relieved I feel when I finish this. Now the snow can melt all it wants, and I'll still be able to take care of her.

I call to her when I'm about halfway up. I'm much earlier than usual. She doesn't sound good when she calls back.

She looks terrible. She's sitting up, and she's licking her shoulder. It looks like she's licked it raw. She's all kind of shaggy and raggedy-looking. She's got foam around her mouth. I take a cantaloupe from my pack and roll it to her. She sniffs at it eagerly, but she doesn't know what to do with it. She hits it, and it flies off the ledge. I say, "Doofus," and take another one out and break it on the ledge.

She's on it in a second and eats it in about four bites. Four very noisy, very messy bites. I roll her another one, and she learns quick. She picks it up and slams it on the floor and then slurps up the mess in about two seconds. I roll her another one. She eats six in a row and then burps. I shoe down again, checking the bolts. I think I've done a pretty good job. I hope so, anyway. Down at the bottom I get the rope. This time, I put on my harness, leave my poles, and only take the rope and the box on my back.

The bear looks at me when I bring up the box, but she doesn't seem too bothered by it. She sniffs it and then walks away. I put it on the right-hand side of the ledge and scoop a bunch of snow into it. She gets the idea straightaway and is eating the snow while I'm still trying to fill the box. I keep getting it on her head. It makes me laugh, and I swear she laughs too.

While she's drinking I go and kick a huge pile of poo off the ledge and feed the rope through the pulley. I let one end of the rope fall, and make the other fast to the harness. Here goes nothing. On goes the belay device, and I snap it to my harness with a locking carabiner and check it four times. Finally, I step out and rappel down. It's a bit funky in snowshoes, but it works.

Now we're getting somewhere. I hook on the huge bag of carrots and hoist it up. I tie off the rope to a nearby tree. I go up again, without the poles.

I think I'm doing pretty well today.

Bear likes carrots. She eats about twenty, and I put the rest of them in her cave. She is already looking better, fluffier. She does a huge wee. Before I rappel down again, I fill up the box with snow. She comes to watch me, hanging her head over the edge as I push up armfuls of wet snow. When I pat her head she shakes off the snow from my gloves and mock-growls. She nuzzles me on my chest, like she likes to do, and I try not to think about teeth.

This close, her shoulder looks really bad. Really, really bad. It smells bad, too.

Now is the time to test my new idea. I rappel down and put the venison in a plastic shopping bag. I tie it off to the rope and haul it up. She looks down at me and over at the bag.

I say, "Go on," and motion with my head. I'm telling her to get the venison for herself. It's the only way it will work.

She just looks at me for a second. "Come on," I say quietly. "You can do it."

Finally, the smell is too good for her. She sniffs the bag and pulls at it, easily snagging the venison clear of the plastic and dragging it to the ledge. She makes a sound almost like purring. I knew she could do it. I knew she could figure it out.

I'm so relieved I sag against the tree.

Now, even if I'm too sick to climb up, I can send up food.

I look up. I don't think anyone would see the rope, not unless they were looking for it. I take off my climbing harness and hook the sled back up to my belt. It's a lot lighter than when I came. But I'm a lot weaker. It's hard to pull.

I have some melons and a bag of apples left under the canoe. It's not enough. I'm going to have to try to find a carcass somewhere. If she were well, she'd be eating a winterkill. I have to try to find a winterkill and bring it to her.

The idea makes me feel sad and hopeless.

I don't know what I'm doing.

But I have to try.

Chapter Eleven

I put the sled in the garage when I get back.

I talk to myself. Sled in garage. Pack with canister under the canoe. I sit on the top step of the porch to take off my snowshoes. And I fall asleep.

I only wake up a little when Mum comes home. She tries to make me get up, but I won't. She gets me to slide up a little on the porch and puts a cushion under my head. She covers me with the green blanket from the sofa. I sleep there until late afternoon, when I get cold. I strip off my outer layer and carabiner it to the bolts on the front of the house. I use the noisy toilet. And then I lie down on the sofa and go back to sleep.

I hear my mother, and I rise out of my body and float

out the door. I see her and Jem, talking. My mother looks as though she might cry.

They begin to go into the cabin. Jem stops and looks at the coat and overalls hanging from the carabiner. He pulls fur from the Velcro fastening of my coat flap.

He makes some excuse to Mum, and then he has grabbed down his snowshoes. He runs, following my tracks. The stairs on the cliff are freshly cut. He sees the bolts in the rock. He sees the half-hidden rope, neatly tied off to a tree.

Now Jem looks as though he might cry. He leans back heavily against a tree. Looks down. Rubs his eyes. And sees something.

It is a cantaloupe. In the snow.

He holds it in his hand and turns it. And then a sound makes him look up.

My grizzly peers down from the ledge. She sniffs the air, complains in her throat. Jem rears back his throwing arm and releases the melon in a perfect pass. The bear snags it out of the air.

I click back into my body. Can I trust what I've just seen? Does Jem *know*?

I see Jem sitting outside on the steps of the cabin for a long time. When he comes in he tells Mum he's sick. He says his head hurts, and that he feels like he's going to throw up.

He doesn't have a fever, and he looks absolutely fine, but he keeps saying he's sick. He skips dinner, and that convinces Mum. But he's not fooling me.

I feel like he's playing some kind of a trick—and like it's a trick *on me*. You get an instinct for it, when you're a sibling. And I wonder again, about my dream and my leaving-my-body thing.

Can I really see things like that? Does Jem really *know*?

Jem has never missed a single day of school. Once, he broke his leg in two places on a Friday and was back at school on the following Monday.

Dad has always been really proud of that.

When Dad gets home and hears that Jem doesn't want to go to school tomorrow, he goes ballistic. He stomps upstairs to examine him and stomps back down. All through dinner, he mutters that the whole family is going to pot.

After dinner I ask Dad about winterkills, saying that they talked about it in bear training. That's all it takes. Pretty soon, Dad has the back of an envelope and is making maps for me to see some interesting ones.

Dad's postgraduate helper arrives tomorrow. She lands about five o'clock, but Dad's going to let her sleep in town. He'll pick her up the day after tomorrow and wants me to go along. It's not a shopping trip, he warns me. But we might stop off in Livingston for a burger on the way back.

Which means I'll need to find a winterkill and get it up onto the ledge. Tomorrow.

I don't know if I can. I don't know if I'm strong

enough to pull it onto the sled and haul it. I don't know if the rope and pulley will take the strain.

I'm in my nice, warm bed. I can see how thin my legs look, even under my duvet.

And suddenly, I know that I can't do it. I have this moment when I kind of pull back and actually think for a moment about what I'm doing. It's totally mad. I just need to tell somebody and let the authorities deal with *a wounded grizzly bear in Yellowstone National Park.*

I roll onto my side, so that I don't have to see my stick legs, but I can feel the logical part of me slipping away. I know I'm not the right person to be dealing with all this. But it's no use. I'm going to try.

I mustn't forget the pepper spray.

I have just become vegetarian.

I will never eat meat of any kind, ever, ever again. I've looked at the three closest winterkills now, estimating how much meat she'll get for each one and how possible they all are to move.

One was not quite frozen anymore, and the smell was so horrible I couldn't possibly touch it. Also, it was full of maggots and flies. How can flies survive when it's so cold every night, anyway? While I was there, the body made this sound, and all this smelly gas came out of it.

That's when I decided on a vegetarian lifestyle.

Now I'm back at the second one. Something has already eaten part of it, but the back end is still there, just now free of snow. There's the head and neck, and then bones where something else has eaten, and then a nice, fresh elk bottom and elk legs on the back. Nothing smells too bad, and there's antlers, which should come in handy for dragging purposes.

It's the one. I unhook the sled from my belt and position it just right. I kind of half close my eyes and pull hard on the antlers.

I expected it to slide toward me. I was going to walk backward, and it would fall into the sled.

But what happens is the spinal cord snaps, and *I* fall backward and into the sled with an old, dead, half-frozen elk head on top of me. I'm lucky not to be gored by the antlers. I scream and kick it off me and run around in a circle, going, "Yuck, yuck, yuck," until I can't breathe and have to lean against a tree, wheezing.

Finally, I calm down. I take deep breaths and try to feel calm and capable. I get a new idea. I will move the sled to the other side and drag the elk's back end into it by the ankles.

It's grosser grabbing ankles than antlers. They squish a little under my gloves. But it works. I now have half an elk on a sled that's tied to my belt. It's the start of grizzly season, and I'm prancing around with a bunch of meat strapped to me. I can't see far in any

direction because of all the trees. And anything could come and eat the elk, and me, at any moment.

Wonderful.

I start to shoe back to the cave, and for just a moment, I think I see a black tail swish behind a tree. That's all I need, wolves. I could pepper spray a bear. I don't think I could hit a whole pack of wolves.

I speed up. That was stupid, because I'm soon out of breath and then have to stop. Every noise I hear, I think it is wolves circling me. My mouth is dry, and my heart is pounding. I don't think I've ever been more anxious. It's a wonder I can breathe at all.

The thing is, I *know* it's stupid to be scared of wolves. I know wolves hardly ever attack humans. But there's all the pictures in my fairy-tale picture books somewhere in the back of my mind, and those horrible scenes in *Beauty and the Beast.* And also, with this half an elk behind me . . . If they were ever going to attack, they'd do it now.

I have to calm down.

I stop and breathe. I close my eyes. I picture my bear, well and happy, running through a clearing full of wildflowers.

Okay. I plodge along in the wet snow. I decide I need a song—not to sing, because that would waste my breath. More like to *think,* so that I can keep a steady, slow rhythm and not wear myself out and get stuck with a bunch of meat tied to me in the middle of flipping nowhere with wolves and grizzlies and god knows what else. . . . There goes my breath again.

Calm. Calm.

And the only thing that I come up with that has the right rhythm is "I'm a Little Teapot."

So I am shoeing along to it. "I'm a *lit*tle tea*pot*/ Short *and* stout"—step—"Here *is* my han*dle*/ Here *is* my spout"—step. I'm picked up and poured out about thirty times before I'm at the bottom of the cliff.

I sit down on a rock and gasp for a while. I swear, when I look at the cliff, it is higher than it was the day before. Finally, I stand up and take off my pack. I've got all kinds of things in there. I look at the elk's ankles again and wish ungulates had proper feet. The hooves aren't all that much thicker than the ankles, and lashing them onto the rope tight enough to stay when I pull up that big rump is going to be tricky.

Finally, I decide on some of Dad's woven bands. I try just one big one, but there's too much give. I use two small ones and hook them to two carabiners, hook those to a big carabiner, and then tie *that* off to the rope with my very best knot.

And I know this sounds stupid, but just when everything is fine, and I'm about to start hauling up, I get really grossed out. It's something about the spine and the way it's broken off and poking out. I can't explain it.

But I have to go off and throw up. And where I go

is where I push over the bear poo, and something has stepped in that, and it smells horrible, and I throw up again.

And then I have to sit back down on my rock because I have black spots. I can't breathe, and my throat hurts, and my mouth tastes terrible, and I can't reach my pack to get my water.

I start feeling sorry for myself. But not for long.

Nobody asked me to do this stupid thing. I got myself into this situation. If I hadn't been so angry at Dad, I wouldn't have gone up the hill in the first place. I wouldn't have nearly killed myself with stupidity, and I wouldn't have sheltered with my bear.

The thought of never knowing her makes me feel grim. I pull off my glove and look at my ring.

A lot of this has been really horrible. But I still wouldn't give it away if I could. I wouldn't rewind and never know her, never understand all I understand now.

I get some water and sit a bit longer. And then I go to the rope.

Chapter Twelve

When I leave my body, I notice something.

Humans always have a lot of things. We cover ourselves in things; we drag things around with us; we use things for a variety of tasks, which would be incomprehensible to any other animal. When we humans stop anywhere, we immediately increase our territory by spreading out our things.

There are a lot of things at the base of the cliff. There is me—a slender human girl, and I'm the disk of the daisy. My things are the petals all around me. The petals are a weird collection—climbing gear, plastic pouches, a sled with half a dead elk, a black jacket with red patches . . .

"Hey," I shout. "Hey!"

I'm answered by the imperative call the bear uses when she wants the girl to come near.

"No," I say, and I'm surprised how tart and bossy my own voice sounds. "You come here."

The bear grumbles. A few moments later the bear's head appears over the edge of the ledge. She sniffs the air, excited by the smell of the defrosting winterkill. She is suddenly very quiet and intent.

"I'm going to haul it up to you," I say. "It's your job to get it onto the ledge."

The bear watches me closely.

"Here goes nothing." I use a bit of metal, and a strap, to make an artificial loop in the rope. I have four or five of these ready on my climbing harness.

I pull with all my strength on the loop, and the carcass begins to rise off the sled. Panting, I raise my knee and put my foot in the loop, and then I put all my weight on the loop. The legs of the carcass start to rise up, but the large hindquarters stay resolutely attached to the sled.

I bounce on the loop. I attach another loop at hand height and pull with all my might while I bounce. Nothing happens.

I say a bad word and step out of the loop. The rope flies up, so that the bottom loop is now hand height, and the top loop is too high to reach, lost.

I say another bad word.

I watch myself sit down and have more water. The water nearly brings me back into my body. I can nearly feel myself thinking.

The bear whines.

"I know," I say. "I'm working on it."

I get an idea. I sink a bolt into a tree, but when it immediately begins to bleed sap, I feel bad, guilty. I know there's a million, trillion pine trees in this forest, but the world needs every single one of them.

I pull off my gloves and work with a rope, some carabiners, and a belay device. I click my harness into the whole contraption. Using my snowshoes and poles to brace myself in the wet snow, I start backing up, and the elk carcass rises.

I am panting hard, panting words. "Pot . . . Stout . . . Handle." I close my eyes for a moment. My face is pale, and I'm sweating. I'm shaking—my knees threaten to buckle.

The elk carcass is three-quarters of the way up the cliff face. The bear swipes at it, as if she could reach it.

Then there is a small cracking noise.

"Crrrrrrr." *I see myself look to see where the noise is coming from. And then I look up, just in time for the* "Rrrrrrrk!"

The bolt zings out of the tree. The carcass plummets back to earth. I am a little doll, thrown hard by an invisible giant into the snowy cliff. I see myself bounce and crash into it again. It hurts. I hear myself scream.

And then I'm gone.

When I come to, I'm back in my body. And I am, apparently, in the middle of a conversation with myself. I blink a couple of times, hearing myself argue with myself and then shake my head a little bit and manage to stop all that.

I'm not thinking straight. That's the problem. I haven't been thinking straight for ages. My shoulder hurts really, really bad, and one of my knees is on fire, and my bikini line is going to be pretty sore from this harness, which I should have taken time to adjust properly. But I didn't. Because I'm not thinking straight.

I'm near the top of the cliff, and the elk half is down at the bottom. I stink of meat. The bear is looking at me, but she's also smelling me. That is not good. This whole thing is not good at all. This is so not good that I don't have any words for it.

And just when I think this, I realize I'm not getting a lot of air and that my black spots have come back. And now it's not a choice.

I float away from myself.

My mother comes out of the cabin and sighs. She opens the door of the garage and sighs. She might even sigh as she starts the snowmobile, but I can't hear it above the noise of the machine. She settles the helmet on her head, slides down her goggles, and rides away.

The clearing is absolutely silent after she goes. The first sound is a flutter of wings. Then there is a little, muted birdcall. Then, one by one, all the little sounds of the forest come back. I can even hear the slight breeze agitating the tops of the pines.

And . . . I think I might be able to do this because I'm a little bit dead.

When I'm a little bit dead, I can float away from myself. And the sicker I get, the more hurt I get, the farther away I can float.

My body is about to be eaten. There's no sense in staying in it.

I might as well float away to our cabin and listen to the sounds the forest makes when there's no humans there to hear. Maybe that's what I'll be, after she eats me and I'm dead . . . something that hears and sees . . . without ears or eyes . . .

Now Jem creeps out and gently clicks shut the door. He peers around the corner at the garage. Then he relaxes—he carries his shoulders lower; he's much noisier. He puts on his boots and snowshoes. He doesn't bother with a coat. He knows where I am, and it's not far away.

He sees all my things first. He stops and looks at them carefully, like he's memorizing the scene, like he'll be tested.

And then he sees me, hanging limp, and my bear, reaching down for me with her giant claws.

He nearly falls over the sled's towline, clambering to the rope. There are two handy loops already attached. He pulls one down, and the elk rises. He puts his foot in the first loop and grabs the second, hauling it down to his foot and standing on it. The elk is now suspended off the sled, and I'm out of the bear's reach.

He removes the first loop and uses it to make a third, higher loop. Hauls again and stands on it. Removes the second to make the fourth. Hauls. The third is now the fifth. The fourth is now the sixth.

The elk is rising. I hear myself say sleepily, "She can get it off the rope if you bring it up."

Jem nearly chokes. He says, "I don't give a damn about the bear."

I say, "I'm okay. My shoulder hurts a bit, and I banged my knee. I'm just tired. I feel really far away."

Now my body weight is being useful. The elk rises easily, and I come down quickly. Jem sits me up in the snow. He is standing in a loop of the rope, trying to detach my harness when the rope begins to shake. It shakes and pulls, but then it is perfectly still, and there is no longer any weight attached to it.

I look up and have that weird, sick feeling from looking both in my body and out of my body.

I close my real eyes and say, "Well, we won't be using those bands again." The torn fabric loops flutter at the top of the rope like miniature flags.

Jem shakes me, hard, by my shoulders. "You little fool," he says. "You complete idiot."

It hurts. I slide down onto the snow.

Jem sits down on the rock and presses the palms of his hands to his eyes. His arms and legs are shaking.

I have to go back into my body. I'm scaring my brother.

"I'm sorry." I sit up. It's easier than I thought it was going to be. I hurt, but I can breathe okay. I guess it's the lying down and resting. I should do that more often . . . like all the time.

Jem is furious. "You've got a pet bear?" He's too scared to shout. He kind of whispers hard at me. "You've got a pet *bear*?"

I get up on my hands and knees and shuffle over to a tree. I'm going to stand. I'm going to pack and get home while I can still hold myself in my body.

I say, "Do we have to have this conversation right now?"

"What?" Jem jumps to his feet. For a moment I think he might hit me. He says, "You did not say that. You did not just say that."

I sit down on the rock. I say, "Look. I've got to clean the blood off the sled and pack up and shoe home and I feel . . ." He looks at me. I know he can tell how I feel.

I say, "I'll talk to you. But I've got to get home. Right now."

He says, "I'll clean the blood off the sled. And I'll haul you home in it. But you've got to tell me what in the hell you are doing."

As Jem cleans the sled and packs up all my stuff, I tell him everything. Absolutely everything. He is utterly horrified.

He keeps asking me questions. He runs back to the house, hauling me in the sled with my legs sticking out all untidy.

I knew he wasn't sick.

He puts the sled away and tucks my bag under the canoe (there's still a bunch of cantaloupe under there) and hangs up our shoes all neatly and everything. Then he runs upstairs and washes without looking like he's washed, and I do some more laundry, putting the special stain stuff that we're supposed to use only sparingly, because of the environment, all over the big bloodstain on my powder-blue fleece. My gloves are caked in blood and sap and things I don't want to identify. I put the washer on the hottest setting and hope for the best.

Mum will be back any moment. Jem told Mum he had terrible diarrhea and then hid all the Imodium. That's how he got her to go to Mammoth.

When Jem comes back down, I manage to put the kettle on. Jem makes me tea and keeps asking me questions. Finally, he sits down and eats four chocolate chip cookies, without saying a word, just looking at me.

I manage one cookie, dunked into my tea. I'm really dehydrated, and the tea is feeling good.

He says, "Let me get this absolutely straight. You nearly killed yourself, and to get warm, you crawled in with a hibernating bear."

I nod, sucking another dunked cookie.

"And then you went back. Why?"

I shrug and then wince. My shoulder isn't broken or anything. But I'm going to have a big bruise. "She saved my life. And I was really sick and unhappy. I don't think I was thinking straight."

"Were you trying to kill yourself?"

The question lies between us like an unexploded bomb.

I can almost see it, almost hear it ticking. And I have to ask myself, *Is that what I do, when I leave my body? Do I play with the idea of being dead?*

Would I leave Jem and Mum and Dad? Would I leave Sue? The idea makes my heart hurt.

Jem says, "Darcy? Were you?"

I say, "No." I try to explain. "I think I'm a lot sicker than anyone knows," I say. "I think I'm kind of . . . not living really well."

Jem looks as if I've hurt him.

"We've all been so busy," he says. "I should have come home earlier more often."

I close my eyes and remember how it was, when I first met the bear.

I say, "It made me feel better . . . being with her. It made me feel more okay about this place. I already felt kind of dead. She made me feel more alive."

I've just talked about her in the past tense. Jem being there today has put her in the past tense. I suppose I already knew we couldn't keep going on the way we were going. Jem has just made me face it.

Jem opens his mouth to say something else, but Mum walks through the door.

"Tea?" she says. "Caffeine? And chocolate. More caffeine. And sugar." She stands over Jem, fuming. She says, "Jem? Do you actually want to go to the hospital? Do you think Darcy's gotten too much attention or something?"

"I really wanted it," Jem says. "I thought I should listen to my body."

Mum hands him the Imodium. "Well, now you can listen to your mum. Take one of these. Drink some water. Lie down."

She smells him. "Have a shower. And *then* lie down."

I feel like a whole weight has been lifted from me. I'll ask Jem what to do. I'll do it as soon as he gets out of the shower.

But of course, I sit down on the sofa. And of course, by the time I wake up, it's dinner.

I forgot to tell Mum that I'm now a vegetarian, but luckily, it's pasta primavera and salad and garlic bread. I don't know what I would have done if it was venison or beef. Hurled all over the table, maybe.

Jem has officially "recovered." Dad is still disgusted about his illness—and mine and, really, pretty much everything. I can tell I'm going to have a great time in the car tomorrow.

After dinner I wash and Jem dries. He says to me, "If you don't come up to my room and talk to me more about this, I'm going to tell Dad."

I say, "I actually *want* to talk to you. I just fell asleep."

He says, "You still look pretty wiped out."

I say, "Thanks a lot."

Just then, Mum says, "I think you should have an early night, Darcy, if you're going with Dad in the morning. You look tired."

Dad looks up from a binder he's making for the postgraduate. He says, "You do. How long were you out today?"

I shrug. "I went to look at winterkills."

Dad's face lights up, and he starts to say something, but Mum pushes me toward the stairs, saying, "Oh, good, that'll give you something to talk about *tomorrow.*"

Jem sits on my bed. We don't know where to start. We're all washed and brushed, and we're just sitting there, looking at each other.

He says, "Her shoulder. How bad is it?"

I think about it. "It smells," I say. "I think she got shot." Although I told him everything, I didn't tell him about my dreams or about leaving my body. I don't know if I'll ever tell anyone about that stuff.

Jem shakes his head. "And she can't get down?"

I don't have to say. He can see it in my face.

It's not until he touches my cheek that I know I'm crying. My eyes are leaking.

Jem says, "Don't worry. We'll think. We'll think of something."

My eyes feel so sore that I lie down and close them. Jem gets up and shuts off my light. At the door, he turns around and says, "Anyway. She's got enough food for a couple of days, at least."

As I'm going to sleep, I realize I forgot to say thank you.

What does happiness mean to a bear? Warmth and a full belly? We're not so sure.

Bears can suffer severe mental health problems in captivity. They pace, they become aggressive, or so passive as to seem catatonic. They lick their fur until it comes away in patches, or they stop grooming altogether. Reproducing is impossible. Self-harm is common.

But other bears adapt well. Those that do, live longer in zoos than they do in the wild. They enjoy puzzles and games from their keepers, and they exhibit moments of joy in their play.

What does happiness mean to a bear?

It depends on the bear.

This bear is a little restless. She has a full belly, and she is warm, but she paces. She licks at her wounded shoulder. At midday she becomes watchful, but in the afternoon, she stretches out to sleep, softly complaining.

My blue polar fleece is completely ruined. I told Mum it was cocoa. Everything else is fine, even my gloves. It's a pity about the fleece because I was going to wear it today. We're wearing jeans and gaiters and jackets instead of snow stuff. Dad has moved the car up the access road and parked it right where the snow ended last night, so there's no need to shoe or hike or anything. Bliss.

I am still totally exhausted, and I'm coughing a bit. Mum wants me to stay home and go to the doctor, but Dad, amazingly, says he thinks I'd be better off going with him. I don't like it when Mum and Dad fight, and from the look on Mum's face, they will. But I do want to go.

So I have on my new cowgirl jeans and an actual top and my rose-colored fleece and my ski jacket, because I'll take that and my gaiters off in the car. I have an actual leather bag and not a backpack. I have on earrings and lipstick. I feel nearly human.

Except for the huge dark circles under my eyes and my vampire-like complexion.

I am asleep the moment we sit in the car. In my dreams I reach out for the bear, but I can't find her. I spend all my dream time looking for her everywhere.

The next thing I know, my dad is shaking my shoulder and I've got drool all down my chin.

My shoulder hurts from sleeping on it, and I stretch.

Dad says, "We're nearly in Bozeman."

I feel great. That sleep has done me the world of good. I get a mirror and stuff out of my bag to sort out the drool and my hair, and I look great too. I've forgotten how nice I can look, sometimes.

Dad keeps looking at me, too.

I say, "Sorry about ignoring you, but I needed that sleep."

He barely answers me, as if he's thinking about something else. Well, I'm used to that.

Dad's postgraduates come in all shapes and sizes. This one, Sally, is blond and Australian and only about an inch taller than I am. She's very bouncy and cheerful.

I sit in the back and listen to them chattering away about bone density and muscle mass and whatever else they're observing. They're copying an observation someone did years back before the wolves came to Yellowstone. There are less deer now, because of the wolves, but Dad thinks that what deer there are, are better deer. That the wolves actually improve the condition of the herd, even as they decrease the numbers.

There's a lot more to it, but it bores me to tears.

We stop for burgers in Livingston, and I eat and eat and eat.

Then Dad asks me a funny question. He says, "Darcy, health wise: How do you feel right now? From one to ten? If one is dying and ten is ready to do a swimathon?"

I suck on the last of my malted shake, and the straw makes a sucking noise. "Umm," I say. "Except for feeling so full that I might burst, I'd say ten."

Outside, Dad says, "Give me twenty jumping jacks."

This is what he used to do to me and Jem when we were little. *Give me ten push-ups. Give me twenty jumping jacks. Do two laps around the garden for me.*

I laugh and give him twenty. He smiles at me, so warm and kind, but also thoughtful.

We all get an instinct for when parents are up to something. My instinct is tingling hard.

Sally sits in the back with me on the way up, and we talk about all kinds of things. Jeans, music, school, my illness. The time she broke both arms at once.

She's lovely and really easy to talk to. But the closer we get to the park, the more I'm willing to just let her talk.

I think I ate too much.

Dad looks back in the rearview mirror at me, and I see him and Sally exchange glances.

My feeling about Dad comes back.

Just inside the gate, Dad stops and takes Sally's picture at the Yellowstone National Park sign at the entrance. Dad makes me get out of the car too.

"Give me twenty jumping jacks," he says on the way back to the car. I just look at him. I want to sit down. My shoulder hurts. My knee hurts . . . actually, every bit of both legs hurt.

Dad holds my shoulders and looks at me. He says, "How do you feel, on a scale of one to ten?"

Sally is looking at me too.

Why are they doing this to me? My lower lip trembles shamefully. I say, "About two or three. Can I get back in the car now?"

I see them talking outside the window, and it's something about me, I can tell.

All of a sudden, everything seems hopeless. Dad and I will never be close again. Sue will forget me. My bear will die of starvation. And me. Maybe I'll die too. Maybe one day I'll leave my body, and I won't find my way back.

Nothing seems to be helping me.

My head hurts, and I want to cry.

Dad gets back into the car. He says, "Honey, I'm sorry, but Sally has forgotten something. We have to go back to Gardiner."

Sally sits in back. She says, "Hey, I'm really sorry. I had a blond moment."

She starts talking about hair, and before I know it, I'm asking her advice about the highlighting kit. I wonder if my hair is light enough to use it. I don't want to have orange streaks. She's telling me all about how to test a small patch and about some of her own hair disasters when we pull into Food Farm's parking lot.

"Can I go in too?" I ask Dad. "Have we got time?"

Jem ate almost all Dad's beef jerky when he pretended to be sick, so that he could save my life. I get a bunch more, so Dad doesn't find out.

They've got vegan food in there, and I start thinking about how my vegetarianism didn't last very long. I grab a six pack of Diet Coke, and a cold one for the road.

Dad is leaning against the car. He says, "If I ask really nicely, would you do twenty jumping jacks for me? I swear there's a real reason for it."

I roll my eyes. I put my stuff on top of the car and do twenty jumping jacks. "How do you feel?" he asks. "From one to ten?"

I say, "I don't know. I'm a little tired. Seven? Eight?"

Sally comes out, and he says, "She did twenty. And she says she's a seven or eight."

Sally looks at me carefully.

"Okaaaaay," I say, looking at them both. "What's going on?"

"That's what we're trying to find out," Dad says. "I think maybe, just maybe, you might be intolerant to midrange altitudes."

I'm sitting up front with him, and we're driving back to the park. He tells me that some perfectly healthy people can't take high altitudes. That usually the resistance point is eight thousand feet, but that for some people, it's six thousand. He thinks I might be one of the some people.

It's interesting at first, but he goes on and on about it. Finally, I tell him that I'm not following him. I tell him that I'm tired.

Sally leans forward with something in her hand. "Six thousand one hundred and twenty," she says.

Now we're back at Mammoth, but Dad doesn't drive down the access road. Sally is going to stay here a couple of days and go through her orientation. Then she'll be in Cooke City, which is the closest town to the cabin. We usually come into Mammoth or Gardiner, though, because Jem's school is there, and Mum gets her mail and uses the WiFi there.

Dad looks at me and says, "You going to get out?"

I shake my head—no. Really, I think I might grab a quick nap. Dad strides off in the wrong direction to help Sally, who is struggling with her bags alone. I'd help, but the idea of opening the car door makes my head hurt. So I close my eyes.

Then Dad is back. He opens my door and says, "Honey, I want you to come with me."

It's the clinic. I don't want to go to the clinic. Then we're with the doctor, and they talk and talk, and the doctor is being really reassuring and nice to Dad, and that seems to make Dad mad, and he starts shouting. And then Sally is suddenly there, and I find out she studied medicine before zoology. She starts using very big words, and I'm on the examination table, so while they're all shouting, I just lie down and have a nap.

I wake up in a hospital bed, but I'm still in the clinic. There's a little plastic clamp over my finger and an oxygen mask on my face. A lady I've seen at the clinic before asks me to sit up, and I take a tablet.

Then Mum is there, getting me to drink my Diet Coke. I must need fluids if Mum is okay with me drinking Diet Coke. It tastes a little flat, but I like it anyway. I drink about a ton of it.

And that's what I do for a day. I sleep, drink Diet Coke, and do a lot of wees. Oh, and I take this tablet.

I see the doctor and Dad and Sally next day. Dad is in his white camo, so he's come straight from the hut. I've already rebelled against the oxygen mask, and whatever numbers are coming out of my finger made the lady say it was okay to remove it.

The doctor has given me a drug that will help with the altitude. There's more he's going to say, but Mum and Dad won't let him. All through the doctor's talk, Dad keeps touching me . . . holding my hand, stroking my hair. He's spent hours in the clinic, and I'm pretty sure he should be training Sally instead.

Unlike the last six rounds of medication, this drug actually makes me feel better. A whole lot better. Dad tells me that Sally's coming to dinner and spending the night, to catch up on her training.

I get to go home, too.

I guess I took for granted the lovely smell of the pine trees. It's so fresh and pretty. The road is open a lot farther now. We shoe in the last little bit to the cabin. In a week, Dad says, we'll park right outside.

It's so good to be back and to be able to breathe. I want to run right up the hill and see my bear. I say, "I'm really stiff. Do you mind if I go for a walk?" Mum and

Dad look at each other for a little while, but then they say I can.

When they go in the house, I sneak back to the side of the porch and take four cantaloupes from under the canoe, bundling them into my jacket.

This will be the last time I can come here without climbing gear. The ledge is over a yard clear of snow.

From the bottom I call, "Hey!" and out she runs. She looks down at me and gives me that bossy *Come here* call.

I nearly run up the hill. But it's tricky at the top. The snow is thin and icy. She's pacing around when I raise my head. I can just get my elbows up on the ledge. I roll her a melon, and her eyes get big and round. She smashes it with one paw, gobbles it up off the floor. I roll her another and another. And then I roll the last one. She's got plenty of water, and there's no big pile of poo.

I stand there and watch her eat the cantaloupe. And suddenly, I realize: *I'm* the reason she didn't come down in time. If I hadn't fed her, she would have had to try harder. And if she had tried harder, and the snow had still been there, she could have come down.

She can't now.

She looks okay, but her shoulder smells really bad now, even from here. She lies down and opens her arm and calls to me, but I don't go. So she comes over and cuddles me, and I stroke her big head. I tell her things.

I tell her about being sick and about the tablet and being better.

And then I tell her that I'm sorry and that I'll think of something to make it better for her.

When I come down, Jem is there, watching me. He gives me a hug, hard and tight. Like he thought I was going to die, or like this is the last time I'll ever see him.

I look at him, and then I look at the trees, and then I look at the cave, and then I look at Jem again.

And suddenly, I know how to set her free.

I tell Jem about it on the way to the cabin. He stops and brushes the fur from my fleece. He takes off my gloves and beats them on a rock.

And then he turns to me and says that (a) I'm utterly insane, and (b) he'd be glad to help.

When we get back I go upstairs to shower and change. After I dry my hair, there's a knock on the door, and Mum and Dad come in. They ask to sit on my bed. They ask me to sit down too.

I think they found out about the bear. Or maybe they're getting divorced. Just when I think this, Mum reaches for Dad's hand. Dad does his deep breath thing that he does when something hurts. He's not looking at me, not properly.

Mum shows me my tablets. It's a twenty-one-day course. She asks me to take my evening tablet and then to count how many days' medication is left.

I say I don't have to count it. It's twenty. One from

twenty-one is twenty. I know I'm rubbish at math, but even I can do that.

Then Mum says, "The doctor won't give you any more. They're not good for you, if you take them for too long."

I give kind of a scornful laugh. I say, "Well, what am I supposed to do? Live happily for three weeks and then feel horrible again?"

Mum says, "No. There's only one cure for acute mountain sickness. You have to descend."

Descend. It means go down.

I have to leave the park.

Dad lets go of Mum's hand and takes one of mine. His voice is clear and calm. He says, "Look. While Mum was gone, she talked to Sue's mum, Mickey." He clears his throat. "In fact, that was why Mum went back to England. To talk to Mickey in person."

When she was so busy. And when I thought she had abandoned me. My heart is so full of . . . feelings. So many kinds of feelings. I think I might just break apart with how many are cramming into it right now.

Dad clears his throat again, and I suddenly realize he's trying not to cry. "Mickey said if it came to it, you could move in with her and Sue. Mickey kind of thought you wouldn't fit in here."

It's so horrible sometimes, getting what you really want.

Moving in with Mickey and Sue? Going home? I

prayed for this. I begged for it. I hated Mum and Dad for not letting me do it last year.

And now that I've gotten it, I don't want it anymore.

Mum stands up and holds me, and I cry a little bit into the soft bit of her tummy. And then I see Dad looking so, so miserable, and I reach out for him, and he stands up and holds me too. I say, "I don't want to go."

Mum sighs. "That's what Daddy said," she says, wiping my eyes with the tail of her shirt. "And I didn't believe him." She holds me hard. "We don't want you to go either," she says. "But you can come back, every school holiday, for three weeks. And we'll be home ourselves, in just over a year."

Dad says, "Some people grow out of it. Some people have it once and then never again. You never know." But I think we all know I'm not going to be one of those people.

It's dark, or I think I'd run outside right now, to get all the time I can before I have to go.

I'll miss my family, but we'll still be in touch.

Forests don't text. Birds and deer and wolves and . . . bears . . . don't post pictures of themselves. I can't believe I have to leave this place, just when I've grown to love it.

"This is probably the worst thing I've ever done," Jem says, sinking the ax deep into a perfectly healthy lodgepole pine tree. "I can't believe I'm doing this."

"You're not," I tell him. "Not really. It's me who's doing it. You're just hired muscle."

It's huge. Plenty long enough to reach the cave. And although lodgepole pines are pretty slim and straight, it seems about as big around as a house right now.

It's sweaty work. Jem stops and wipes his face. "I don't think the rangers would buy that," he says. "Here, you. Time to get the saw."

Lots of the cabins have old tools in their sheds. Ours has this two-man saw, neatly nailed to the wall. We'd taken it down and oiled and sharpened it. I hope nobody notices it's missing.

It's a bit tricky to use, but once we get the rhythm going, it doesn't take long to saw down the tree.

When it cracks and starts to fall, we watch it go, just like Jem said it would, slowly, slowly down to the ledge.

The bear is not impressed. She shouts in alarm.

I say, "Hey, doofus! It's a bridge!"

The top of the tree just about fills the ledge. Suddenly, she pushes her way through the branches to look at me. Her face is so expressive. You can tell she's thinking, *What have you done now?*

Jem and I can't help it. We start to laugh.

"What the—" Tony has appeared out of nowhere. His face is pale. He looks at the saw, the ax, and the tree. He says, "Why did you kill a tree? How *could* you?"

And then he sees the bear, pushing her way through the branches.

He's going to start shouting. He's getting red splotches on his cheeks.

Jem says, "Keep quiet, Tony."

Tony is shaking—with fear, maybe. Definitely with anger. "What in the hell?" he mutters. "What in the hell?"

Jem takes Tony's arm and starts pulling him down the trail to the cabin.

Tony tries to shake him off.

Jem just drags him away. He is talking low and calmly into Tony's ear.

I can't see them anymore. But I can hear when Tony begins to shout at Jem. I can hear him say, "About a million regulations."

All the noise is making the bear nervous. She goes back into the branches and hides.

I sit down on my rock. It's cold sitting on rocks without overalls. There's a lot of blue sky, but it's going to rain tonight. Dad says almost all the snow will be gone tomorrow. He's going to service our bikes when he gets home.

I tell this to the bear, like we're having an ordinary conversation, like it's a normal feeding day.

I wish she'd come out. I wish she'd come down.

I'm a little bored.

I start singing. "I'm a little teapot/Short and stout./ Here is my handle/Here is my spout."

She pokes her head out again. Sniffs for the boys. I tell her they're gone.

I go to the base of the tree and pat it. I move my head like she does, when she wants me to come close.

She whines. She paws at the tree, as if she could push it away. She probably could, too, if both arms were working properly.

"Stop that," I tell her. But she doesn't get the fact that it's a bridge. She thinks I've done something really stupid instead of something terribly clever. And then, I know: I'll have to show her.

It's not easy to get up on the splintered base of the tree and climb onto the trunk. I guess it's not a trunk anymore; it's a big log. Anyway, it's a big old thing, and I have to scramble and kick a bit before I'm on it. I start walking up. It's rock steady. Jem's done an excellent job, just like he does at everything. I hope he's not fighting with Tony. I hope he's not getting arrested.

The bear looks at me, interested. I walk up a bit more. It would be good if I had on climbing shoes instead of Sorels. It would be good if I was roped in somewhere. It would be good if I'd had a bit of a brain working before I got us into this mess.

I can tell when she suddenly understands.

Her eyes widen, like they do for a cantaloupe. She looks at me and at the tree, and at the ground, and at me again, and she whines a little and gives herself a shake.

And then she starts pushing through the leaves to get onto the log.

Which is great, which is just what we want. But it makes the log rock a bit, and I nearly fall.

So I sit down. It's too big to ride like a horse, but my center of gravity is lower when I'm sitting than when I'm standing, and I can kind of surf the shocks.

She starts to come down forward, like an idiot.

"Turn around," I tell her. I'm sure she doesn't understand, but she does it anyway. She turns around and starts kind of shinnying down.

She's grunting in pain, but she's fast. She's very fast. I push myself back until I can jump down. I get a bit away. I don't know what she'll do.

Will she cuddle me?

Will she eat me?

When she comes down, she stops for a moment, and licks at her shoulder. She looks up at the cave and all around her. She gets up on her back legs and sniffs the air.

And then she just walks away. Without a backward glance. I see her big shaggy bottom for a little while, and then the trees swallow her up.

My bear is gone.

I sit back down on the rock for a second.

Last night my heart was so full of feelings I thought it would burst. But this has left me feeling totally empty. Of course I didn't mean to her what she meant to me. Of course she has a life to be getting on with.

I realize I've got stuff to do too.

I pick up our things, kick dirt over the fresh-looking scar of the tree, and head back to the cabin.

I search my feelings, but I don't feel anything.

Maybe a bit of relief.

Maybe a bit of emptiness.

But really, nothing.

Chapter Thirteen

Jem has made a pot of tea. Tony looks at me and then looks away.

I want to walk right back out again.

I say, "She's down. She's gone."

Tony talks in the coldest voice I've ever heard. He says, "You've just let a wounded, food-dependent bear loose in the park. Well done, Darcy."

His voice has made my eyes sting. I say, "She can get her own food now."

"Her own carrots and cantaloupes?" He bangs the table with his fist. He says, "She's habituated, you idiot. She'll hurt somebody."

There is a long moment in my head, where suddenly, I see—really, really clearly—something I probably should have seen all along.

I just hadn't thought—hadn't thought of that at all. And I can tell Jem hasn't either. It's the kind of thing you don't think about, I guess, unless you live there. Unless you think about stuff like that your whole life.

"I don't think she will," I say. "She's not like that."

Tony says, "Oh, that's good. I'll just bet my little sister's life on that. Because Francesca is playing outside, right now, not even four miles away." He stands up and starts pacing around the room. He looks at me. "Didn't you listen in the bear orientation session? Didn't you hear any of it?"

Jem says, "Calm down, Tony," and pours me a cup of tea. He adds the milk, and pushes it to me with a couple of chocolate chip cookies. But I can't eat or drink. I feel sick inside, and stupid and small and unworthy.

I stare down at the table.

Tony sits back down. He says, "Right. Here's what we're going to do."

Big drops of water are falling on the table. They're from my eyes. My nose starts to run, and I sniff.

Tony says, "Don't snivel. We don't have time for it. Your parents will be back in a few minutes, and I need to get home."

He sighs. He says, "Look. I'm going to radio in seeing a wounded bear. That should get the word out, so that people take precautions." He runs his hand through his hair. He points at me and then at Jem. "If there is any news of that bear approaching humans, you are going down to the station and telling them everything."

We nod. I say, "I'm sorry."

But he ignores me.

When Tony stands up, Jem does too. I hear Jem say, "Thanks, man." There's a moment, and then Tony punches Jem on the arm.

I look up, just for a second, when Tony leaves, but he doesn't even glance my way.

Then Jem is back. "Drink your tea," he says. "You're pale again."

Without my tablets, I could have just slid into sleep.

Instead, I drink my tea and go up to walk around my room. I'm done with this park.

Tony hates me. I've put Jem in a bad position. And I've probably screwed up my bear. I think that's it. I think that's all I can wreck.

I get down my suitcase and start packing.

I don't sleep that night, and I can't read. I look out my window, as if in the five million acres of wilderness, my bear will choose to walk into the little square I can see. The rain is pouring down. I can actually see the snow fading into the earth.

Toward dawn, I get out my computer and look at all the bear pages again. How could I miss it? "Feeding a bear is not kind—it is a death sentence for the bear."

"Food-dependent bears must be destroyed." "Once a bear is habituated to human contact, especially to human food, it becomes a nuisance bear."

Maybe she'll just forget. Maybe she'll just get on with being a bear and forget all about the ledge and me.

Dad sees my light and comes into my room. It's stupid o'clock, the time he usually gets up.

I'm crying a little, and he comes to cuddle me.

He says, "You mustn't get too down about this. You can come back for three weeks before school starts."

I say, "I can never come back here—never, never, never." And I cry really hard.

Dad pulls away and looks at me, like I really am a horrible teenage monster. I want to tell him that it's not because I don't love it here. I want to tell him everything. But I just can't. I can't.

He goes to work thinking I hate everything he loves.

Jem comes in and holds me tight. He says, "We were both dumb. It's not just you."

But it is.

We have a graveled driveway. Who knew? I've never seen it before.

I cycle down it, with my phone, charged, in my pocket and onto the access road. Mum says if I feel that good, I might as well go to school. But there's no point, and we both know it.

Sue's mum, Mickey, is a teacher. She's already said she'll catch me up on all I missed. And school is different here, anyway.

It feels really good to ride a bike. I'm miserable and feel sick to my stomach, but I can't help but notice that I feel like I'm flying. Tony and Jem were whooping this morning when they left for school. Now I know why.

Sue and I have both been sleeping with our phones under our pillows. It's late back home, on a school night. I can picture Sue in her bedroom, see her asleep with all her teddies stuffed around her (I am sworn to secrecy about Sue's teddies).

The phone tower in Mammoth is by a big parking lot. I sit right on a bench about twenty feet away from the thing, and I still only get three bars of reception. But at least I know I can call her number. And at least I know she'll answer.

"Darcy? What time is it?" She is always grumpy when she first wakes up.

Just hearing her voice makes me start to cry.

"What's wrong?" She's not grumpy anymore. "What's wrong, Darcy?" I can picture her nightgowns. I can practically smell her, the special smell of a million sleepovers.

I say, "Raisin flapjack." Which is our code word for "I've totally messed up." It's a long story.

I can hear Sue sit up. "How could you raisin flapjack? You haven't been doing anything!"

Somebody is making a noise behind me. It's a noise

I've heard before, and I don't pay any attention to it. I put my finger in my other ear and start to talk. I tell Sue everything. She asks me questions, usually to explain things, now and then, but she just listens.

I know it sounds weird, but I can *hear* her listening. I can hear her just listen, and I find it very comforting.

I finish by saying, "So she's out there, somewhere, probably just about to attack somebody. And Tony won't ever speak to me again. And my dad thinks I'm a total jerk, and I can't explain anything to him."

Sue is quiet for a moment. She says, "You really have raisin flapjacked. But how cool is that, Darce? Sleeping with a flipping bear?"

I sigh. I look at my ring. I say, "Yeah, I know."

We're quiet for a moment. Then Sue says something that really stuns me. She says, "I'm jealous."

I don't say anything. I don't believe it.

She says, "I know you've been really ill and that you've messed up. But you've done so many exciting things. You've seen wolves and bears and climbed up cliffs and stuff."

I say, "When I come back in August, if I'm not banned from the park for life, and if I'm not in jail, you'll have to come with me."

"And meet Tony?"

"Tony hates me now."

Sue says, "You have to tell your dad. You have to tell him everything, and he'll help you."

I shudder. "He'll kill me."

Sue makes a little impatient sound. "Your dad loves you. I mean, really loves you. That's another thing I'm jealous about."

Sue's dad is a hideous waster. He's in the music business and thinks he's really cool. He's always canceling their time together. He once called *me* Sue, because it had been so long since he'd seen her, and when he'd turned up out of the blue at their house, I was downstairs.

Sue says, "Babes, I've got to get some sleep. But don't worry. This is the kind of thing your dad knows about. All you have to do is get him to listen."

I say, "Love you."

She is sleepy. She says, "Love you more."

I'll bet she dreams about my bear.

I am so sad and so kind of *wrecked.* It's all been too much, being so ill for so long, and the bear, and . . .

I've been so stupid.

I wish I could leave my body again. I wish I could fly away and know if my bear is safe.

I don't really go, but I get this feeling . . . this kind of hungry, desperate feeling. I don't think she's okay. I don't think she's okay at all.

When I come back to myself properly, I'm sitting there, looking out at the kind of gritty, gray earth that's around the hot springs. There are chipmunks everywhere, and they're really cute.

The sound behind me has stopped, and just as I

think I'll turn around to see what it is, Tony comes and sits on my bench.

He says, "I don't hate you."

He has a skateboard under his arm, and his black hair is flopped in his face. He's wearing slim-legged jeans and Vans and a long-sleeved T-shirt. He looks wonderful.

I say, "How much did you hear?"

He says, "Hey, I was skating. I only heard the end because it was my own name. It's not like I was listening."

I shrug. I say, "You know everything, anyway." I fiddle with my phone for a moment and then slide it into my pocket. "By the way, why aren't you in school?"

He says, "I always cut classes one afternoon in spring, so I can skate this lot before the tourists arrive."

I turn around and look at him, look at him properly. He smiles at me and then skates off. He's good. He does some tricks, plays around on some ramps. He's really good. I can tell; I've seen loads of skaters at home.

I sit with my arms around my knees, watching Tony Infante skate.

When he comes back over, I tell him about the half-pipe in the park at home. He says, "When I go to college, I'm going someplace like that. Most of the towns around here have a bunch of rules about skating. It's hard to find a place where I can meet other skaters."

We look at each other for a long time, until it gets awkward and we suddenly look away. And then Tony says, "How are you feeling? You want to go and get a Diet Coke? The store's open."

Tony tells me about what the rangers said about the bear. I tell him about her shoulder and how bad it smells. We're quiet for a while.

And then we talk about other things.

We talk about August and how the summer people have a big Christmas party on the twenty-fifth. Tony and Jem are going to work in a kitchen, they think. They put in their applications that morning. They'll be able to go to the employee pub and all the free movies and dances and things.

I say, "You'll probably meet lots of girls."

He says, "You'll probably meet other skaters."

We look sideways at each other and smile. And it feels good.

And suddenly, I wonder if we'd even be able to talk so . . . kind of clearly about this kind of stuff, if I hadn't messed up so bad.

Tony says, "You were really stupid."

I say, "I know."

And then he says, "You were righteously brave, though, Darce."

And something amazing happens. I smile, and Tony leans forward, and so do I and . . .

It doesn't last long. But it's really special.

We wait at the access road for Jem. It's a long climb

up from school. We all cycle home together. The boys don't mean to, but they race far ahead of me. It's time for my tablet. I can feel it in my legs.

I think about my bear, ill and hungry, out in the woods somewhere.

The rangers said that she might get desperate for food. They've alerted everyone in the area. They think it's a shame she's so close to Mammoth and Cooke City. Tony says because she's wounded, they'll just kill her.

My dad is home when we get there. He's writing up notes again and has papers spread everywhere. Mum has driven in to the library but will be back soon.

I take my tablet. Jem and Tony go up to Jem's room.

I decide to make some chocolate cupcakes. It only takes about half an hour. I make frosting while they cool, and I put the kettle on. I make Dad tidy up his stuff. When Mum comes home, I call the boys down, and we all have a nice cup of tea with my cupcakes.

Dad says that Sally will be here soon. She's coming for a meeting and staying for dinner. Just as he says it, she's here. Early.

I get another cup.

Sally kind of bursts in. She starts talking before she even gets in the door. She's seen a bear.

Everyone's kind of tolerant about her enthusiasm.

We pour her some tea. She says it was so close to the little hut that she saw it hunt a calf. Or try to. She says the bear's shoulder was a "real mess."

Suddenly, the boys and I are really listening.

Dad asks, "What do you mean, a real mess?"

Sally says, "She's got herself a bad wound. It looks infected. I think it looks gangrenous." She drinks some tea and takes a cupcake, adding, "She looked sick."

Dad says, "Sounds like the one you saw, Tony, hanging around here."

He gets the radio and calls the rangers. Sally reports what she saw, and you can hear the guy on the desk kind of sigh. He says, "She sounds like a situation ready to happen. Just in time for opening day for the hotels."

He thanks Sally.

I go upstairs to use the toilet, but then I just lie down and sleep.

Chapter Fourteen

In my dreams, I float loose of my body and go into the forest to look for her. It is dark and quiet. Billions of stars pepper the sky with little points of light. The moon is fat and yellow above the trees. In my dream, my dream body can talk. It calls, "Hey. Hey, Bear."

Now I can suddenly smell my way through the pines. The whole forest has become a scent-scape. I can smell the warm earth, the green, pealike odor of pushing plants. I can smell how each tree has its own resinous signature.

I am looking, looking for something, for someone. With my nose. I am smelling trees and rocks and earth, looking for a molecule of scent; a slight trace that could become an inky flood of direction.

And then I catch it. I catch it with a strong smell of oil and rubber. I follow the rubbery smell down a wide path with, increasingly, many small stones, to a wooden structure that smells of men.

I wake up in the dark. I put on a fleece and my slippers and go downstairs.

I know she'll be there. I'm not at all surprised when I open the door.

She gives me that *Come here* sound, and I do. She rubs her face on my neck and chest, and I pet her, rub her ears.

She is hot. She is hot, and her eyes are runny, and she smells horrible.

She's really sick.

I go into the cabin and get a big mixing bowl and fill it with water. She drinks it all, and I go into fill it again, and she drinks all that too. And then I go in again, and I give it to her again, and Dad is standing there on the porch.

He doesn't ask me any questions. He just stands there and watches me water my bear. It makes me a little clumsy to be watched like that, and I spill a little.

She ignores him. She's so thirsty.

I stand next to her and look at Dad. I say, "She's sick."

He says, "I think she's dying."

It's not like I didn't know that already . . . but when Dad says it, it makes it real. I feel my knees quiver, and I sit down on the bottom step of the porch to watch her drink. She doesn't really notice Dad is there. She lies down at my feet, and I stroke her face.

I have tears running down the back of my throat. I'm choked with sadness.

Dad says, "I have a feeling this is a long story."

I nod. I say, "I've been stupid."

"Are you the one who shot her shoulder?"

I say, "No!" and she growls a little. I say, "No. She's always been this way." I look at her. I say, "She's gotten a lot worse since she woke up."

Dad comes and sits by me, and she doesn't even mind. He reaches out and strokes her head. He says, "Bears' metabolisms slow right down when they're hibernating. It probably slowed down the infection."

I look at him. I say, "I love her."

Dad puts his arm around me and holds me tight.

He says, "She's got blood poisoning, I think. Gangrene and sepsis is a horrible way to die." There's a moment when we both look at her. He says, "Sally said she was only using three legs." He doesn't come right out and say that nobody can make her better. He can tell I know that, that I've kind of known that all along.

I also know what he thinks I should do. I say, "I don't want to call the rangers. They'll be all gung-ho. They'll scare her."

Dad puts his arms around his knees and thinks. I love how Dad can think like that, with people watching. He thinks for a long time, and I lean against him. She's not asleep, but she's close to it. I can feel her pain almost like another person with us.

Finally, Dad says, "Do you feel responsible for this bear?"

I nod miserably. I say, "I fed her." It makes me choke a little to talk, and I'm not sure he can hear me. "I didn't know how stupid it was, but I fed her. I think that's why she came to me now. She's hungry. I . . . could kind of feel her being hungry. . . ."

I don't want to go into the whole leaving-my-body thing. There are some things you really shouldn't tell your parents. I don't think Dad would ever be able to sleep again if he knew I'd been dancing between life and death. The bear thing is bad enough.

His face is hard to read. He stands up, and she opens her eyes and looks at him in a kind of careful way. It reminds me that she's still got those claws and teeth and is still strong enough to use them.

Dad looks down at his feet, almost like he's bowing to her. I can hardly see his face in the shadows. I've got no idea what he's thinking.

Then he slowly backs into the cabin. Lights go on, and I hear him moving around. The bear loses interest in the cabin and its sounds.

She looks far away. I wonder if she's leaving her body, too. I wonder if that's what happened to us. We both kept leaving, and we got mixed up when we came back.

I can't stop touching the fur on her head. Even though she's hot and it's greasy. It's all kind of a miracle.

When Dad finally comes out again, he has got my boots and overalls and coat. He's already dressed.

He has also got a rifle.

I say, "You aren't going to shoot her, are you?"

"No," he says. "You are."

The problem is, she doesn't want to go anywhere.

It's only when I remember the cantaloupes that I get her to her feet. There are four left. I stuff the other three down my coat and hold one out to her. She lumbers to her feet and follows me. She's using all four legs, but she's limping badly.

It's so bizarre, leading a bear through the woods. With a cantaloupe. With my dad.

The stars are bright, and there's zillions and zillions of them. There are stars you'd never see anyplace else but in the wilderness. The pine trees are exhaling, and the smell is rich and clean at the same time.

I'm walking with my dad and an actual grizzly bear, through the woods, in the night. Every once in a while, I actually think about what we're doing, and I get this little bubble of . . . of pure life . . . that just comes up in me.

We go along the trail, and when she looks like she wants to stop, I bowl her a melon.

The bear is having fun, too, I can tell. It's something about being with me, about not being alone anymore. It's not just the food or the water. I don't know how I know, but I know.

"She's still pretty fast," Dad says, starting to jog a little. "I'd rather wait until we get over into the national forest to shoot her." He looks back. "And I'd rather we didn't actually get mauled before we do."

I say, "I don't think she'd ever hurt me."

He says, "I'm kind of depending on you being right about that."

Dad feels the life bubbling up, too. It's sad and it's illegal, and it's utterly mad, but my dad is enjoying it. I look back at the bear. I remember when I was the weak one and she was the strong one.

Now, I have my tablet and can jog along like this and still breathe. And my bear is really sick and hurting. Suddenly, I can feel how badly she's hurting. I look back, and she's only using three of her paws.

I say, "I'm going to give her another melon."

I have two left, and they're bouncing around all over my chest, banging in and out as I run. I've decided I don't want big boobs anymore if this is what it's like.

Bear eats this one fast. Her breath is coming hard. I tell Dad we have to slow down a little. She's got some of that foamy stuff going on around her mouth.

He says, "Not far now."

There's no line or fence or anything. When we get

there, Dad just knows where we are. He leads us to a big meadow. It seems warmer here than in the pines. I can still see hundreds of stars in the lightening sky, little silver fairy lights in the pale gray ceiling. The new grass smells strong and fresh.

I feed Bear the last cantaloupe. She licks up every little bit and then comes and sniffs at my chest.

"No more," I say, and open my coat and fleece.

She sniffs my top, and I pull that up too. And then she sniffs my tummy and licks it with her rough tongue. I laugh and pull down my shirt.

Satisfied that there's no more melons, Bear flops down on her bad side. Dad stays a little bit away, but she keeps on ignoring him. I don't know why. Maybe he smells like me. She's just not interested.

She raises her good arm and calls for me, and I can't help it. I have to go to her.

Dad makes a kind of strangled protest when I lie down and slide into the bear's arms. I'm too far away to see his face, but even from there, I can see his hands shaking. But there's nothing he can do to stop me, and there's nothing I can do about it either. I've already made my choice here.

The bear reaches out and pulls me into her body, and I lie in her arms.

She is terribly hot, and her bad arm smells worse than it ever has before. I can feel her sigh. I tuck my head down, and she rests hers above it. She holds me so gently. Even though I can kind of feel her claws through my coat, I'm not at all afraid.

I think of all the times we've been together. How she saved my life. How I tried to save hers.

She moans a little, but I know she is asleep. I can feel the rhythm of her breath against my own ribs. She's gone dreaming. Perhaps she's floated free of her body. She might be looking down at me right now. I turn a little and look up at the sky, pretending I am looking back at her.

I want to stay forever. I know, in a way, I will always be here, lying in the arms of this bear.

Chapter Fifteen

"Darcy," Dad says. It's all he has to say. There's a whole lot he puts into my name. He's got new feelings about me. He's also terrified.

I open my eyes and slide out from her paw.

Dad holds his arms open wide, and I go from the bear holding me to my dad holding me. He seems, for the first time in my life, little. It wasn't just his hands—I can feel his whole body trembling.

I suddenly realize it has been really brave of him, letting me do this. Letting me lure a bear with food and cuddle a full-grown grizzly. That he has . . . trusted me.

And I haven't cried all this time, but this thought makes tears come out of my eyes.

When he lets me go, he hands me the gun. He says,

"The safety is off." He points to a place on his own head. He says, "Don't put it against her, but shoot her here. She'll die straightaway."

I start to walk toward her, but he stops me. He gets out his radio and turns it on. He sends out a call, asking if anyone can hear him. He says we're just across the line in the Gallatin, stargazing, and that we're being followed by a female grizzly. He says she's limping and that she's exhibiting aggressive behavior. He turns the radio off again, without waiting for an answer. He says, "Now."

It's only a few steps from Dad to the bear, but it feels like it takes me years to walk it.

The gun is cold and heavy. I have to hold it high or it will drag on the ground, because I'm so small. *I'm too small*, part of me thinks. I'm too little to do something like this. I should ask Dad to do it.

But then I think Dad has done enough killing.

I know I can't do this. But I have to do it anyway.

I stand and look at her for a second. And then I put the rifle against my shoulder, and about four feet away, making sure I don't pull to the left, I pull the trigger.

The noise is deafening. I bend over her, and you can hardly see where it went in. But below her head is a spreading dark puddle. You'll be able to see where it went out.

All the air in her lungs comes out of her mouth in

a big whoosh, and I breathe it in. I don't mean to, but I do. I was breathing in anyway, and it just comes into me.

I hold my breath. I hold her inside me. I can feel it, so warm.

And then I breathe her out, free, into the cold night sky.

She was so beautiful. She was so very, very beautiful.

Dad is there. He gives me a can of pepper spray and tells me what to do. Then we sit down in the grass, and he tells me what to say. Over and over, he tells me what to say.

My eyes are leaking, and he keeps holding on to me, but I can't really feel his cuddle. I can't really feel anything.

He turns the radio back on. And we start walking back to tell Dad's story.

We were stargazing, we say. Dad carried the rifle because we were going into the national forest, and, like many of the men here, he always carries it when it's not illegal. We were lying back in the grass, looking at the stars, when a grizzly came right for us. We tried to get away, and we thought we had. That's when Dad turned on the radio. But she heard that and came after us, so Dad turned the radio off. I'd been holding the pepper spray while Dad used the radio, and I sprayed her, but she was so desperate, it didn't stop her. So Dad shot her. She was almost on us when he shot her.

That's what we say. We say it over and over and over and over at Cooke City, as the sun comes up. Then this young woman in a suit comes running in and says the Yellowstone rangers found tracks, and that they think the bear followed us from our cabin, that she was stalking us.

Her radio crackles, and she talks on it to the Yellowstone rangers. I worry that they're going to say something about finding bits of cantaloupe. I wonder if we remembered to put away the big bowl I used to water her. I look down at the Velcro around my wrists to make sure we got all the fur out of it.

But nothing like that happens. They stop questioning us, and we sign a few forms and go home.

Mum is utterly horrified.

Jem has taken off another school day and stayed with Mum. He hasn't told her anything. When we get home, she thinks we've been attacked by a bear.

Finally, even though it's only about eleven in the morning, Dad chills and then opens a bottle of white wine. He makes about a hundred big toasted cheese sandwiches and opens one of those huge bags of potato chips, and we sit and drink white wine and tell Mum what really happened.

Then she's even *more* horrified.

I start from the beginning and tell the whole story.

Mum keeps telling me how stupid I was and how lucky I am to be alive. When the bit about the elk's spine breaking comes, she makes a face like she's about to vomit.

But Dad's really into the whole thing. He laughs so hard when I tell him about the bolt shooting out of the tree and me slamming into the cliff face that he spits bits of sandwich everywhere.

He puts another bottle of wine in the fridge, even though Mum tells him off.

Before Dad opens that, we all go down to the cliff with the climbing bag and some other stuff. Dad and Jem use a fallen tree as a lever and roll the big one Jem had cut down away from the ledge. Dad goes up and rescues his pulley and rope and what's left of the big plastic storage box and the carrot bag. He also inspects and tidies up the bolts, which he says he'll leave. He says the cliff will make a good climbing gym, and he's right. There's loads of handholds and footholds now that all the snow is gone.

Mum goes around the side and buries the bear poo. And that's my mum all over. She's still muttering to herself about what I've done. But she deals with it.

I say, "By the way, that hat you're wearing?"

She looks at me, eyes narrowed under the band of the lilac hat. She says, "Yes?"

I say, "I cuddled the bear wearing that. And I wet my pants when I was wearing it. And I haven't washed it."

She shrieks and pulls it off her head, and it almost lands in the bear poo.

She tells us she hates us all, and we laugh so hard I have to sit down on my rock and gasp. I watch her while she fiddles about with dirt and dead pine needles, trying to hide the poo burial artistically. Dad and Jem are messing around on the cliff, arguing about routes up. I close my eyes for a moment, and let the sun come through my eyelids.

When we get back, we have showers, and then Mum makes chicken samosas, and she and Dad and Jem drink the other bottle of white wine. We carry the table out onto the porch and eat out there. It's a really special day. We finish off my cupcakes and drink pot after pot of tea.

Mum keeps giving out these little screams whenever she thinks of me in the cave with a wounded grizzly. Dad roars with laughter when she does it. He's a bit like a bear himself. I'm surprised I never noticed.

Then people start coming by, bringing us food. Tony's family. Nancy and her husband. Sally. A couple of rangers. The guy who taught me bear awareness.

This is what the gung-ho nutcases do when something like this happens. Mum told me it was a bit like this when I first went into hospital. They had about fifty casseroles delivered. Their whole social life, she said, seems to revolve around helping one another survive.

She sounds cross when she says it, but I can tell she's happy that they are starting to fit into the life of the park.

Everybody brings a bottle of wine or something to eat. People are all over the house, sitting on the canoe, the porch railing, the sofa, the floor. The table on the porch is groaning. Mum keeps bringing things out. It's like the parties you have after a funeral. People tell bear stories. Sally tells her story about twenty times. She's excited by the whole thing.

Jem has already had two glasses of wine. Dad winks and pours me a tiny one, but I don't really drink it. I don't think it would do well with my medication.

Suddenly, I feel really, really sad. For me, it really *is* like a party after a funeral. And I can't join in with the laughing and joking.

Dad comes over and puts his arms around me. He whispers into my ear. He says, "She couldn't have lived, sweetie. You saved her a lot of suffering."

I know he's right.

But still.

Jem and Tony and I walk down to the base of the cliff, and we tell him the real story. The way Tony's eyes are shining at me, I wish Jem would leave us alone together. But he doesn't.

Oh, well, I think. There's always August.

And Christmas.

And Easter.

We get a moment, walking back, when he takes my hand and squeezes it. "You did the right thing."

I can feel my heart pounding hot in my chest.

I say, "Well, it was stupid feeding her in the first place."

Tony grins. "Well, yeah," he says, and bumps his shoulder into mine. "Really stupid."

Jem really doesn't know what's going on. He's walking ahead of us and can't see Tony holding my hand. He says, "Oi, Infante, be nice to my little sister."

Tony kind of smiles and then says, "If you insist," and squeezes my hand again. My heart is so hot I think it might melt my shirt.

It's a good feeling.

The last days whip by. Before I know it I've got two suitcases and a backpack in the car, and Mum is driving me past the sign that says LEAVING YELLOWSTONE NATIONAL PARK.

I undo my seat belt. Mum makes a small disapproving sound. I twist in my seat, looking out the back window at the trees and the mountains.

I can't believe how much it hurts to go.

It's not just my family I'm leaving behind. It's part of myself. Or maybe I'm not leaving part of myself behind. Maybe the wilderness has become part of *me.* Maybe I'll carry this place with me, wherever I go, just like I carry Mum and Dad and Jem.

I can almost see down into our valley from here, and farther than that is the meadow where she died.

I'm not going to be the same. I'm never going to be the same.

I have to catch up on my exam work and do nearly two years of study in one. I'm going to miss my family horribly. I'm in love with a boy who will be three thousand miles away. But none of that seems too difficult to handle.

I strap myself back into the passenger seat. Mum gives me a look, but she doesn't tell me off. Before, she would have given me a lecture on car safety. I guess, after everything that's happened, I'm probably not going to hear many more of her lectures on car safety.

I remember the day I set my bear free, and I wonder if Mum will feel that horrible empty feeling too, when she waves me through security at the airport. I wonder if she used to feel it when she said good-bye to Dad, when he went off on army missions, or the day she first watched Jem snowmobile away through an icy forest.

I say, "Don't worry. I'll always wear seat belts properly. I'll look after myself."

She keeps her eyes on the road and nods. "Good," she says briefly. And I feel all the other things she's not saying and all the tears she's not crying. She says, "You'll be all right." Because that's what we say, in my family.

I'm asleep on the transatlantic flight. I can feel the jet rumbling underneath me, flying through the night, under a thin coating of cloud.

I fly out of the jet, and go back, back. I am running through a meadow with a giant bear. The bear chases me, tackles me, pushing me down into the tall, soft grass. The bear wraps her arms and legs around me, and we roll, over and over.

In my arms the bear grows smaller, lighter, thinner, until she is a cloud of a bear. I suddenly find it hard to breathe. I lie in the grass, gasping, and the bear swims into my open mouth and disappears inside my body.

I wake up, into that strange combination of noise and quiet you get on a long-haul flight. My ring is cold and solid on my finger, like an anchor that holds me in my body. It's also like a warning to the whole world that I might be only small and thin . . . but there is a bear inside me.

Author's Note

When you live in grizzly country, you think about bears. You think about them when you go for a walk in the woods. You think about them when you plan a picnic. You think about them suddenly when you've run out of the house at night to get something from the car and hear a rustle in the dark. . . . I lived in the Greater Yellowstone Ecosystem for six summers and one winter, and I thought about bears the whole time.

When bears climb into your mind, I don't think they leave it again. I still dream of bears.

The bear in this book is based on Bear 134, a grizzly whose territory was next to the hotel where I worked. I saw her hundreds of times. I even watched her teach her cubs to fish. If she hadn't been sleepy the day I almost stepped on her head, I might not be here today (wild strawberries—neither of us could leave them alone). I saw her mate get cross and charge a line of cars and cameras. I saw her swim. I saw her gnaw on a half-frozen elk carcass. I scanned for her with a zoom lens and fell over backward when her huge teeth filled the viewfinder.

And one day, more than twenty years later, she was suddenly there for me again, just when Darcy needed her.

I hope she'll always be there for you, too. I hope you dream of bears and take the bear inside you, to remind you of your own strength and beauty.

Acknowledgments

I would like to thank everyone at Wendy Lamb (especially Wendy Lamb and Dana Carey) and all at Random House Children's Books. Their editing has been exquisite. I'm also indebted to Oxford University Press and all the amazing people there.

My agent, Sophie Gorell-Barnes at MBA Literary Agency London, has represented me for many years, and I owe her many thanks for her patience and kindness.

The Lighthouse Writing Group—Tanya Appatu, Emma Geen, Susan Jordan, Sophie McGovern, Peter Reason and Jane Shemilt—are all talented writers and share their writing lives with me. I can't tell you how warm and wonderful that is.

Bath Spa University and the Royal Literary Fund have supported me during the writing of this book. I am extremely grateful to them for providing me work that allows me to support my family and still pursue my craft. I'm also very fortunate to have amazing writers as my daily colleagues.

And finally, I have to thank all my friends and family for putting up with my neglect, especially Joan, Sue, Annemarie, Sam, Alison, Deidre, Kim, Hope, Barb, Bryan, Mom, Andy, and Libs. Thank you for not giving up on me when I go deep into my cave.

About the Author

Mimi Thebo is an American writer who lives and works in England. This is her first book for young people to be published in America. Her work has been translated into twelve languages, adapted for film by the BBC, and illustrated in light. The *London Times* called her work "empathetic and humane" and described her style as "spare, yet poetic." She thinks good fiction can change the world.